OUT OF SIGHT

A TRUST ME NOVELLA

TRUST ME SERIES
BOOK 4

MARY ELIZABETH SUMMER

MONOCEROS
PUBLISHING

1

THE HOTEL

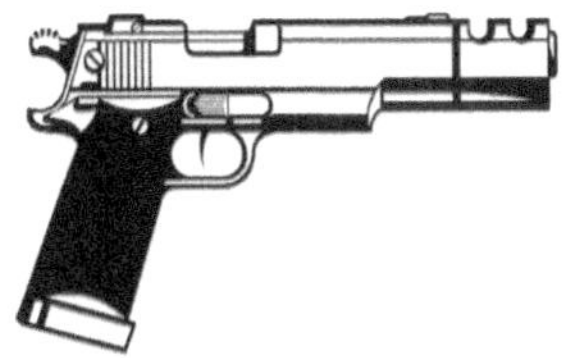

*G*oodbye, *milaya.*

Dani removed the slide from the frame of her Glock 19 with a comforting snick. She always felt safest when the gun was in her hands but broken down into harmless pieces. It was close enough to reassemble and use if necessary, but with no intent in the moment to harm another. She examined the barrel with meditative attention. The cleaning ritual calmed her. The smooth feel of the gun and the repetitive movements quieted her mind. Kept her worries at rest, if only for a moment.

Do not look for me.

Not that the occasional painful thought did not creep in.

She took a cleanish cloth and wiped the slide rails. The cloth came away as tarnished as her soul. She may not be serving Petrov of her own free will, but she still served.

Live your life.

The part she could not reconcile was that she had bargained for Julep's life with more than her own. Did Dani really have the right to sacrifice untold others to spare one person? And yet, she would not make any other choice, were she forced to choose again.

Be happy.

Dani sighed and reassembled her gun. She pushed herself wearily to her feet, wincing as her injured arm twinged a painful reminder of yesterday's session with Petrov. He called it training, but it was really punishment for Dani's betrayal. She had chosen Julep over loyalty to him, and he would never allow her to forget it.

Stowing her Glock in her shoulder holster, she walked to the window. Edging the green curtain aside, she scanned the perimeter of the twilit parking lot. Petrov had ordered her to rendezvous with him at the motel but had not said when he expected to arrive.

So much useless waiting. It had been months since she left Chicago under Petrov's command. Months of constant traveling with him, knowing nothing of his plans. Her only purpose now was to keep Julep out of Petrov's crosshairs. If she could do that, then it would be worth it.

The door to her room opened, admitting Andriy, one of Petrov's more loyal enforcers.

"Any word from Petrov?" Dani asked, resuming her seat at the table under the ochre lamp.

Andriy grunted noncommittally and tossed a takeout container onto the table next to Dani's elbow. She did not want the food, but she forced herself to eat it anyway. She did not know when she would be given the opportunity again.

She opened the container and grabbed a piece of greasy chicken with her fingers. The chicken tasted faintly metallic from the gunpowder residue that had transferred to her hands, but she barely noticed. What was a little extra brimstone to her?

Julep's face that last day in the hospital flashed into Dani's mind like an afterimage. She dropped the next bit of chicken she had been about to eat back into the container and got to her feet, heading to the kitchen to wash her hands.

The phone in her pocket vibrated against her hip. She wiped her hands on a fresh towel that perhaps had once been white and pulled out the phone, expecting to see a message from Petrov. Instead, an unknown number appeared on the screen. She unlocked the phone and opened the message.

Meet me at the tree.

No indication of the sender's identity, but none was necessary. She deleted the message and pocketed her phone.

"I am going out," she said, gingerly pulling her jacket over her injuries.

"Boss won't like it."

Dani ignored this observation as she pocketed an extra mag of ammunition. Knowing Han, she would likely need it. Then she pulled open the sticky motel door and strode out into the brisk night.

Petrov had kept them on the move—Vienna, Kinshasa, Beijing, Bogota—more cities in three months than Dani had visited in her entire life. He seemed to be amassing contacts, settling supply lines, brokering deals, and bribing politicians. Dani was never privy to the strategy behind these efforts, but she had the distinct impression that Petrov's interests were no longer his own. He would leave the room when a certain person would call, even when he was in the middle of a training session.

The orders from the mysterious stranger took Petrov's crew to every corner of the world. And just a week ago, those orders had led them back to Chicago. The ache beneath her ribs intensified the closer she was to Julep. Sticking to her promise to stay away had been far more difficult this last week than it had been in the three months since she had walked out of the hospital.

She arrived at a bus stop and sat on the bench to wait. A few minutes later, a бабуся in a threadbare scarf and a man's overcoat joined her. The woman's face was so wrinkled that her eyes crinkled almost closed when she smiled.

"Storm's coming," she said, taking a seat on the bench next to Dani.

Most strangers took one look at Dani's black jacket, her tattooed neck, and her forbidding glare and made a number of assumptions—all of them accurate. The brave ones who attempted conversation were usually disappointed in Dani's lack of response, and vaguely threatened enough to move away quickly. But this woman reminded Dani of someone from Ukraine, a grandmother who had occasionally given Dani and the other сирота scraps of bread and kind words.

"It seems clear," Dani responded, glancing at the few stars strong enough to break through the light pollution that blanketed the city like a smoky, neon fog.

The woman tapped her own chest with a gnarled finger. "Storm's in here," she said. "Been brewing since last Thursday."

Dani nodded as if this made sense. "What happened last Thursday?"

"My son left for the war."

Dani did not know which war the woman meant but it did not matter. The ravages of war were the same on hearts and minds regardless.

"Your storm has been brewing for longer than that, though, hasn't it, дочка?"

Dani started at the word *daughter* coming from the woman's lips.

"What?" she said, her skin prickling with unease.

"Your storm is locked inside an iron chest, wrapped in chains, and secured with a thousand locks. Storms aren't meant to be locked away like that."

Who was this woman? Was it a coincidence that she spoke Ukrainian? Did she know who Dani was?

"Storms aren't meant to be locked away like that."

"I... I cannot... My life is not mine."

She shook her head dismissively. "Your heart may not be yours, but you always have a choice."

"I do not understand. Do I know you?"

"No," she said, as the bus Dani had been waiting for pulled up to the stop.

The woman rose unsteady to her feet. She shuffled to the bus as the driver opened the doors. At her beckoning gesture, Dani realized that she had yet to move. She hurried to join the woman, prepared to help her climb the steps. But that was not the woman's intent. Instead, she waved Dani to board the bus ahead of her.

"Unleash your storm, дочка. You will be unstoppable."

Then the doors of the bus closed, leaving the old woman on the curb.

"Wait," Dani said, turning to stop the driver. But when she looked back, the old woman had disappeared.

2

THE BOOKSTORE

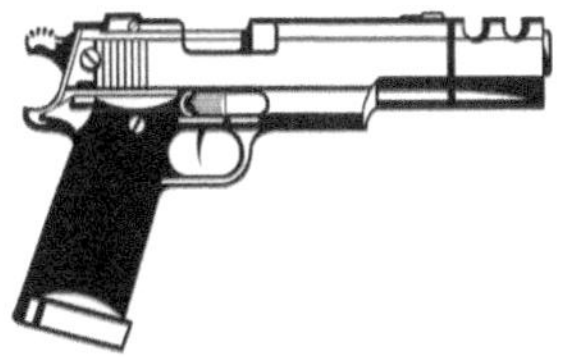

The "tree" that Han had demanded an audience at was not, in fact, a tree. It was a bookstore. Specifically, the Magic Tree Bookstore in Oak Park. Seeing the familiar green awnings and white logo brought back memories of both comfort and guilt.

"Been a while," Han said, appearing out of the shadow of the doorway as Dani got off the bus. "I'm surprised you remembered the way."

Han looked as flawless and beautiful as always, her shimmering black hair in a tight ponytail. Her dark brown eyes glittered with an internal fire that consumed anything that stood in her way. A volcano. It was difficult to resist her when she wanted something, and she had wanted Dani from that first day three years ago—Han working enforcer detail for the Triads, Dani having just arrived with Petrov in Chicago. It had taken Han a while to wear Dani down, but she eventually succeeded. They were together for two years, one of them good, one of them not. And then Julep had grifted her way into Dani's life, making it impossible for Dani to stay.

"I presume your invitation was for more than just a social visit?" Dani said, deciding it was better to get straight to the point.

Han's expression held more bitterness than welcome, but she led Dani inside and to the furthest corner of the store, where they would not be heard over a rabble of children participating in a read-along.

"I need your help," Han said, her gaze troubled. "I wouldn't ask if I had anyone else."

"I know. And I owe you for helping me with—"

"Stop," Han said, her voice rippling with warning. "Don't say the name."

Dani acquiesced, falling silent, while Han shifted to the side to compose herself. When she turned back a moment later, her enforcer persona had slipped into place, and Dani let out the breath she was holding. No scene this time. No gun, at least.

"I need your help," Han said again, perhaps trying to restart the conversation.

"I am bound to Petrov," Dani said. "I am limited, but I will do what I can."

"I know," Han said. "The syndicates are gossiping like a bunch of aunties about the Ukranian's return. How did he get out of prison?"

Dani did not know, though she had suspicions. "He tells me only where to go, who to target, what to acquire. I suspect he works for someone else now, but I do not know who."

Han shudders. "I can't imagine who would be powerful enough that Petrov would agree to work for them."

"I will find out if I can."

"I don't care about that," Han said, her features twisting. "I have bigger concerns right now."

"What concerns?"

"It's easier if I show you."

Han swiveled to the shelf on her left and tilted a blue, cloth-bound book at an angle. A click sounded. Then she pushed the shelf forward, revealing a hidden room. She stepped inside the dim interior, looking over Dani's shoulder to make sure no one else was watching.

Dani followed her into the gloom, though with Han's temper, Dani could not be entirely certain that Han did not intend revenge. She was clearly still angry and hurt, though Dani had broken off their relationship nearly a year ago. But what actually awaited them was far more shocking.

Three small children huddled around a tablet, its flickering glow the only source of light in the closet-sized room. The children were silent in a way that Dani recognized at once.

"What is this?"

"They're Uyghur. Siblings. Escaped a People's Republic internment camp with help from a low-level official who risked his own safety to rescue them."

"I have heard of the internment camps in the Xinjiang province, the assimilation programs," Dani said. "But how are you involved? Why are they here?"

Han shifted uneasily from foot to foot, not meeting Dani's gaze. "I can't tell you that."

"Who brought them here? Are there others?"

"I can't tell you that either."

Dani raised an eyebrow at her. "Why ask for my assistance if you cannot tell me anything?"

"I need your help relocating them."

"Why?"

"I can't—"

"—tell me that. Of course." Dani sighed heavily, running a hand through her short hair in mild exasperation. "What is the job?"

"They need to be taken to O'Hare, but not the main terminal. There's a hangar on the east side of the tarmac. A security guard in a red turban named Karanveer will meet you at the gate and take them from there."

"Why can you not take them? You are the better choice. You know where to go and who your contact is. You know who to reach out to if something goes wrong."

"I'm being watched."

Han looked frightened, which was not like Han at all. She had been trained by the Triads from a very young age to fight, to kill, to use her fear to fuel the inferno inside her. She had also spent two years in the People's Liberation Army, flying combat air missions for the Ground Force. She did not scare easily.

"I suppose you cannot tell me where they are headed."

Han shook her head. "Even I don't know that. Each leg of the journey is kept isolated from the others to protect everyone involved."

Dani nodded, the familiarity of the strategy sending a prickle of unease down her spine. Petrov had used a similar tactic for his human trafficking business.

"Will you do this for me?" Han asked, her shadowed face more fragile than Dani had seen it since she had ended things between them. It was a measure of her depth of feeling for this project—or perhaps these children—that she pleaded rather than demanded. Dani owed her a favor, and this was barely a delivery errand, despite the delicate cargo. But Dani had no doubt already missed her rendezvous with Petrov, which meant additional consequences. Did she really want to involve herself with this, given her situation?

"I am sure you have other contacts who could have assisted you. Why ask me?"

Han stuffed her hands in the pockets of her bomber jacket and leaned back against the closed door. "There are others I could ask, but...after what happened with Petrov and the Ukrainian girls..."

"You believed I would care about them," Dani realized aloud.

Han did not confirm it, but she did not have to. She was right. Dani would care about the children, perhaps more than most others in their profession.

The children had turned from their tablet to regard Dani and Han with a calm resignation that spoke volumes. They were of varying ages. Two girls and a boy, maybe twelve, ten, and seven. Dani wondered if they even knew how old they were. Time in such conditions is a completely different construct than time in the rest of the world. Dani still was not sure how old she herself was, though she had crafted a response to the question that suited her well enough.

The girls had long, dark hair bound in braids. The boy's hair was trimmed short around his ears. They each wore Nike sweats in neutral colors. The youngest clutched a small, stuffed unicorn with giant, gold-flecked eyes in the crook of her arm as if her life depended on its presence. Dani thought of Julep and smiled softly in solidarity. She, too, knew how it felt to have her existence depend on another.

Dani knelt next to the girl. She wished she had something to offer them. Tatyana had always favored the корівка fudge candies that Dani would steal from Амстор. But they were not in Ukraine now, and Tatyana could be anywhere or nowhere at all.

It was the boy who approached first, his features carefully schooled to hide emotion. She extended her hand palm up, halving the distance between them. The boy looked to the older girl, as if silently asking for permission to engage. Regardless, the girl did not tear her cautious stare away from Dani to either consent or refuse. She seemed by far the more skittish of the two. The boy must have come to a decision on his own, though, as he placed his cool hand in Dani's. Dani clasped the small hand gently and shook once before letting go.

"What are you called?" she asked them, but they stared back at her blankly. To Han, Dani said, "They speak no English?"

"No. Only Putonghua. It can make explaining things to them challenging. But they don't resist. They are like living corpses." She shivered as she said it, but she straightened, flipping her hair over her shoulder to cover her lapse of composure.

Dani inhaled deeply, the smell of books thick in the close air.

"I cannot be away from Petrov long. But I should be able to take them to the airport."

Han's smile when it lit her face was like the sun rising from behind a mountain. Dani felt a stirring of nostalgia, remembering what it was like to wake up to that smile. Han had always been the most beautiful woman Dani had ever seen. She just...was not Julep.

"Thank you," Han said, taking a step in Dani's direction as if wanting to hug her, though she seemed to think better of it. "I can't tell you how important this is to me."

Dani nodded. "If I do this, then our debt is paid, yes?"

"Yes," Han said, her smile cracking at the edges. "Just to the airport."

Dani nodded, already mapping in her mind the road ahead.

"I will need to borrow a car."

3

THE AIRPORT

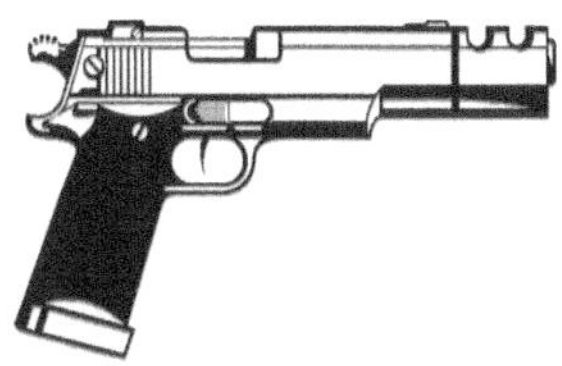

"Sorry. It's all I could find on short notice," Han said, though she did not sound particularly contrite as she exited the driver's seat of a Toyota Cressida that was easily ten years older than Dani.

"It has wheels and fuel," Dani observed. "And it is unremarkable, which is to our benefit in this case."

"I suppose that's true," Han said. Then she spoke to the three children in Putonghua.

As they huddled together under the streetlamp, listening to Han's instructions, Dani studied each of their faces. The only sign of life among them was the smallest girl clinging to the eldest's hand. This favor was going to be both easy and incredibly difficult.

Han opened the backdoor of the Cressida. The children climbed in without hesitation. Their unquestioning compliance resurrected an old dread in Dani. She had seen similar submission in the girls Petrov had imprisoned. After freeing them, Dani had hoped never to see its like again. She had been foolish to think she had cured all the worlds' evils by eradicating one. And how could she think she had eradicated it at all, if she was serving the same man again?

Han handed her the keys. "Don't go anywhere but the airport. There are people looking for them. Bad people."

"Do you know why?" Dani asked, though she did not really need to know to accomplish the mission.

"I can't—"

Dani waved her to silence with a wry smile as she sank into the driver's-side seat. "I will leave the car at Chengdu," she said.

"Dani..." Han trailed off in uncharacteristic hesitation. She never hesitated, *especially* when she was unsure. She usually spoke like she was throwing darts. But now she fiddled with the weather-stripping on the edge of the car door, looking anywhere but at Dani.

"Yes?" Dani prompted. She needed to get moving. Petrov was likely already looking for her.

Han finally met her gaze, her dark eyes liquid with emotion. "I wish..."

Dani felt the aching misery in those two small words, knowing full well its origin: that Dani would not do this *for Han* but instead to counter a debt owed to Han *by Julep* and in part because Dani harbored a weakness for children in distress. Dani had said yes for every reason *but*

Han, and the truth of that hung in the air between them like a blade about to fall.

Dani saw it play out on Han's aesthetically perfect face, and she simply had no idea what to say. Julep would know. But Julep was not here. And if she were, it would make Han's pain a thousand-fold worse.

"I will keep them safe," Dani said softly. It was all she could promise.

After a moment, Han nodded curtly and stepped back, allowing Dani to shut the car door.

Dani drew her seatbelt up and out as far as it would go, then looked over the back of her seat at the children. She waved the hand holding the belt buckle while looking straight at them, saying, "Put yours on," and hoping they understood. Then she buckled hers with the loudest click she could manage. She looked over the seat once more to see each of them mirroring her action.

Good. This was going to work. Probably.

She pulled away from the curb, watching Han watch them leave in the side-view mirror. Then she turned her eyes to the road ahead. Twenty minutes to the airport. Just twenty minutes.

Unsurprisingly, twenty minutes goes fast when you are constantly scanning all visible intersecting roadways for signs of pursuit. No pursuit showed itself, however, and their tiny troop arrived at the airport with a comforting lack of excitement.

Dani circled the airport a few times to be absolutely

certain no one had followed them before turning onto a frontage road leading to the hangar Han had indicated.

She parked at the back of the hangar, pulling alongside the shadowed edge of the building. There were no other cars at the hangar, which could mean that Dani's contact had not yet arrived, or it could mean something else entirely. The only way to find out would be to exit the car. She did not wish to bring the children into an unknown situation, but nor did she think it wise to leave them in the car unprotected. She unbuckled her seat belt.

"Come with me," Dani said, gesturing to the car door. "Out. With me."

The children sat very still and stared unblinking at her.

She sighed and got out of the car. Then she opened the boy's door, gesturing for them to come out and stand next to her.

The children did, though they eyed her distrustfully. At least they were showing some sign of emotion now. Perhaps it meant they were open to the idea of trusting her eventually. Not that it mattered. They would soon be on an airplane to another destination. Dani hoped it was better than where they were now, that it was far better than where they had been before.

She drew her gun but left the safety on, carrying it down against her leg to keep from frightening the children. With her other hand, she gestured them toward the nearest door. They dutifully headed in that direction.

When they reached it, though, Dani waved at them to stand to the side so she could open it with her sight-lines clear.

She twisted the knob, waiting for a lock to catch, but none did. The door swung outward an inch, and Dani scanned the interior as much as she could through the crack. When nothing dangerous jumped at her, she opened the door a degree wider.

The interior was dimly lit, both fortunately for their own ability to avoid notice and unfortunately in that it granted the same cover for everyone else. Nothing appeared out of the ordinary, though. The hangar housed a small biplane, likely meant for short excursions only. If there were four seats in total, Dani would be surprised. Regardless, her contact did not appear. Perhaps he was in the pilot's seat already?

She led them cautiously through the door, gun still down as no threat presented itself, and circumscribed the perimeter, all three children trailing in her wake like silent ducklings. No sound, no lights, no movement. Her shoulders relaxed fractionally, though now that her eyes had adjusted, she scanned the dimness with more care.

Dani led her troop over to the office, which was no bigger than the room behind the bookshelf had been, but with a desk and two chairs and a windowed wall. Was it perfect cover? No. But it let Dani see without necessarily being seen first.

The children took seats to wait, the youngest squeezed

into the chair next to her brother. The sight of them bunched together reminded Dani so strongly of Tatyana and the other сирота that it took her breath away. She had not realized how much she still missed them.

The door on the other side of the hangar from them opened, and a man wearing a red turban walked in. He seemed unconcerned with stealth, so the hangar must have been territory he was familiar with, and he must not suspect imminent danger. Both were good signs. She straightened, holstering her gun, and waved at the children to stay where they were, holding a finger to her lips in what she hoped was a universal gesture for *keep quiet*. Then she let herself out of the hangar office, closing the door behind her with a click.

The turbaned man turned at the sound, a smile blooming on his face. He looked young in the dim lighting, though his beard held a fair amount of gray.

"Greetings," he said in accented English. "I suppose you are here to deliver the children." He looked around, clearly noting their absence. "Where are the children?"

"Safe," Dani said. "What is your name?"

"Karanveer, brave and kind warrior of the Khalsa, at your service."

The name matched the one Han had given. Still, Dani preferred to be thorough.

"May I see your identification?"

"Of course. It is commendable to be cautious in these matters."

He took out his wallet from a pocket in his security uniform and pulled his driver's license from the windowed slot. He handed it to Dani, along with the security badge he had clipped to his shirt pocket, for closer inspection. Both pictures looked like him, though in the dim interior she could not be sure. Dani handed the identification cards back and decided to trust him, more because her instincts told her she could than because of his ID.

"The children are in the office," Dani said. She signaled through the window for them to come out.

"They are so quiet," Karanveer observed to Dani sadly as they walked over. "Children should only be this quiet when they sleep."

Dani agreed. She and her friends, though they suffered, had been boisterous and full of life. These young ones were far too guarded.

"Why are you doing this?" Dani asked without consciously meaning to.

"The Khalsa are defenders of religious freedom. We fight injustice and persecution wherever we find it. As for why I myself am fighting this particular battle, well, that is a long story, my friend, with a few...events...that are quite unpleasant for me to recount." He paused, caught in a moment of anguish. "I venture to assume that you have a similar answer to that question."

"I am here only to do a favor for a friend."

"Perhaps," he said with a sad smile. "But you are here all the same. And I sense that we have much in common."

Dani nodded. "I would like to know what—"

But before she could finish, several windows shattered inward at once, spilling a tidal wave of faceless operatives in black into the hangar.

4

THE SEWER

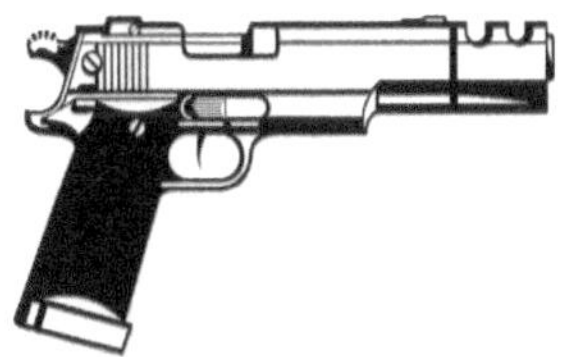

"Raba sānū bacāvē," Karanveer muttered like a prayer, pulling a knife from his pocket. Then to Dani, he said, "Take the children and run."

Dani pulled her gun and pivoted to position the children between herself and Karanveer.

"Run!" the Sikh warrior said again. "There are too many of them."

He was right. Even under cover, they would be surrounded in less than a minute. But she could not leave him completely undefended. She straightened from her defensive crouch and offered him her gun.

He shook his head. "I am more of a threat with a gun in my hand. With only a knife, I can keep them at bay with less of a chance of getting shot myself. Go, now.

There is a drain shaft leading to the sewer in the wash bay at the back."

"Thank—"

"Go!"

So Dani went, holding her gun low, and urging the children ahead of her with gentle nudges. She kept close to the ground and behind shelving wherever possible. She had no idea what a wash bay was, but she knew sewers.

She glanced over her shoulder at the sound of men shouting behind her. They surrounded Karanveer, guns drawn. The Sikh fighter dropped and rolled in the opposite direction from where Dani had led the children, coming to his feet near a strut supporting a platform of tools. He loosened a length of thick chain tied to the post, causing the platform to tip, and a pile of heavy equipment to crash down on the intruders' heads. Then he leaped into the airplane and started its engine, flashing its lights, no doubt to cover the children's escape.

Dani took full advantage of the distraction, shepherding the children to the wash bay as fast as she dared. She found the drain shaft at once. The grate that covered it was screwed into place, so she wasted precious moments locating a tool that could work the grate loose. Shots rang out behind her, causing the oldest girl to flinch badly. The boy flung his arms around her, and the youngest clung to Dani's leg. It would not be long before Karanveer yielded one way or another to the greater firepower of the enemy.

Dani redoubled her efforts, scraping the pads of her fingers against the screws as she worked them out of their sockets. Finally the last one gave, and she thrust the grate aside, lowering each small body in turn to the metal ladder fastened to the concrete just below the opening.

"Hurry, hurry," she said to them, hoping they understood at least that much.

The boy climbed down the rungs in the narrow shaft. Dani was not certain the rungs were meant to be handholds, but the apparatus appeared to bear the children's weight well enough. Perhaps it would hold for her as well.

Dani climbed into the shaft after the smallest one, pulling the grate over her head. Wiggling her fingers through it, she screwed two of the screws back in to delay their pursuers if they tried to give chase. Then she slid down the ladder, skipping as many of the rungs as possible, until she hit the cement below. Her injured arm throbbed hot, but she ignored it.

The children huddled against the far wall, waiting for her and eyeing the tunnel with naked fear.

"It is okay," she said in a hushed, calm voice, kneeling to their level and taking the eldest's hand. She offered each of them a reassuring smile. "I am at home in these sorts of tunnels. I know what to do."

The youngest relaxed first and approached her, leaning into her shoulder. Dani cautiously put what she hoped was a comforting arm around the young one's narrow shoulders.

The boy looked as if he would like to cry but tears would not come.

Suddenly, the young girl let out a piercing shriek that ricocheted off the cement walls around them.

Dani jumped up in alarm. "What is it? What happened?" she asked as she checked the girl for wounds with frantic hands. But there were none. The girl's distress only increased as Dani failed to find the source of the problem, and soon the sound would bring their pursuers straight to them.

The boy tugged Dani's jacket sleeve as the girl continued wailing and pointed back up the ladder. Hooked to the top rung was the stuffed unicorn that the girl had been carrying.

Dani wasted no time. She flew back up the ladder to retrieve the toy. If it would keep the young one quiet, it was worth the lead time lost. When Dani climbed back down and returned the unicorn, the girl stopped wailing at once and hugged it to her chest.

"We must go," Dani said anxiously. Karanveer's actions may have distracted their pursuers, but after the girl's echoing cries, Dani would be a fool to think them safe. Especially if their pursuers had managed to capture Karanveer alive.

Dani led the children through the dry tunnels for perhaps a quarter mile, taking turns at several junctures to throw off any pursuers. Dani let her sense of smell lead the way. Following air freshness quality when wandering storm drains had not once led her astray.

After several such turnings, she stopped them in an alcove to rest and make a new plan.

The children sank to the floor quickly, eyes closed, breath deepening. Dani doubted they were deeply asleep, but she was glad to see that they knew when to take advantage of a chance to rest.

Dani, meanwhile, pulled out her phone. There were no signal bars this deep underground, but there was a weak, unsecured wifi signal coming from an establishment above them.

She quickly tapped out a message to Han. *Airport raided. Handoff failed. With children in sewer. Advise.*

She leaned back against the cool concrete, and for the first time allowed herself to speculate about who these children were and why they were so important.

Dani knew a little about the plight of the Uyghurs. They were a religious minority in China that were heavily persecuted by the current government regime. She had no idea why the People's Republic had singled out the Uyghurs specifically—the real reason, not the religious excuse—nor did she know the true conditions the Uyghurs were subject to, though she had heard enough. But none of what she knew explained why a government official had risked his life to rescue these three specific children. Nor why the government leaders had committed such resources to retrieve them.

The youngest rolled over in her sleep and lost hold of her unicorn again. Dani reached over—slowly, so as not to startle the girl if she woke—and replaced the now somewhat grimy, stuffed toy back into its mistress's arms. The child did wake then and blinked up at her. Dani raised her hands to show she meant no harm and slowly returned to her previous seated position.

The girl laid on the ground a few more minutes, not moving, during which time Dani turned her attention to her phone again. Still no cell signal. But the message to Han seemed to have gone through. She should just turn the phone off. Save the battery. She might need it later.

But before she could do so, she felt tiny fingers slide over her hand toward her phone. Dani stiffened, trying to keep still, but the girl did not seem to notice or care. She simply melted against Dani's side, eyes on the bright, rectangular screen Dani held.

Dani shifted to make room for the child. Then, rather than stare blankly at the screen, waiting for a text that may or may not come, Dani navigated to something more entertaining.

Julep had once said that cat videos were the closest thing to a universal language. And Tatyana had loved cats when she was little. So Dani searched YouTube for a compilation of cute cat videos and tapped the play button. The wifi signal seemed strong enough to support the video stream, though not terribly well. The video paused to buffer for a few seconds before starting again.

The girl—Dani had begun calling her Tatyana in her head—was instantly captivated. And even Dani felt herself relax a little under the furry tyrants' relentless adorableness. So much so that, before long, she had slipped into a light doze herself.

When Dani awoke some time later, it was to a stiff neck, aching bruises, and three warm bodies curled up next to her, watching videos on her phone. They did not cringe away in fear when she moved, which she supposed was progress. It would be far more helpful if they were suddenly able to speak Ukrainian or English, or if Han appeared with fresh resources, or at least another plan. But Dani would take what she could get.

Dani gently pried their little hands from her phone and looked for a return message from Han. Nothing. She should probably try calling Han instead, but for that, she would need to get to the surface. Then she noticed the now red battery-life indicator.

"It is running out of battery," she told them. She assumed saying the words was useless, but perhaps they understood the battery icon.

She turned off and pocketed the phone as she stood, gesturing for them to stand as well. They followed her without complaint, and for once they watched with curiosity rather than blankness.

She led them further down the tunnel, angling them as far away from the airport as she could without going in a straight line. She estimated they had traveled about three miles to the southeast of the airport.

A short while later, she found a hatch with a serviceable ladder. She gestured for the children to wait at the bottom as she scouted the exit.

The sewer let out into a forested park. Dani did not recognize it, but then she never spent time in parks. Still, it was a relief to know that she would not have to usher the children out of an opening located in a busy intersection or barricaded behind an impassable privacy wall. She would take trees over a padlocked alley gate any day.

She returned to the children to help them climb up. It was not a short distance, and it was the middle of the night. The children were exhausted by the evening's events, and, frankly, so was Dani. She supported half Tatyana's weight as well as her own as they squeezed up the narrow ladder, side by side.

When they finally emerged into the park, the children's fear seemed to return, and they huddled together, eyeing the trees around them with concern. Dani replaced the sewer cover, and then turned to them, kneeling to their level.

"I understand you are frightened. But it will be all right as long as we stay together, yes?"

The boy straightened as if preparing for an unpleasant task, but he wore a determined expression. Dani could feel the same determination coursing through her veins. These children deserved safety and a positive outcome, whatever that was for them. Dani refused to allow any other fate to befall them.

She pulled her phone out of her pocket, pressing the ON button, but nothing happened. She pressed the ON button again, but still the screen remained dark. It must have run out of battery after all. She swore under her breath in Ukrainian, pocketing the now useless phone. They would have to find another way to call Han.

"Come," she said to them, placing a hand on Tatyana's shoulder. "We must keep moving."

5

THE CHURCH

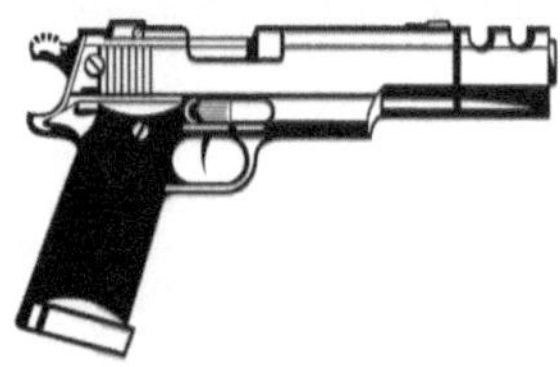

Dani was not sure which direction led to a street, but she figured uphill was more likely, as downhill often led to water. So uphill they went through the thick brush and tall trees until they came across a dirt path that wound through the undergrowth. Dani nearly tripped in the darkness. The older girl—Nadia, Dani had decided to call her—had reached a hand out to steady her. Dani squeezed it gently and held onto it as they broke through the brush onto the trail.

At nearly two in the morning, the path was all but deserted. The people who did happen to pass did not seem likely to have mobile phones, so Dani did not ask. She kept her ducklings close as they followed the path without incident to a park entrance.

Then it was Dani's turn to hesitate. The relative safety and anonymity of the densely wooded park was much preferable to the unpredictability of brightly lit streets, cameras at every intersection, and no transportation. Her hand itched to draw her gun, but she left it holstered under her jacket.

She needed to contact Han for new instructions. A borrowed phone would do. Or a charger. But not many businesses would be open. Still, any direction was better than none, so she picked one at random and started walking.

A block and a half later, Dani was about to alter course toward a larger street in hopes of finding an open convenience store. But as she took a step in that direction, she felt a tug on her sleeve from the boy. Dani looked to where he pointed to see the golden domes of St. Joseph floating above the buildings.

"It is a church," Dani said.

The boy, who still needed a temporary name—Oleksiy, maybe?—tugged her toward the church. At first, Dani resisted—they needed a phone, not intercession. But the boy was insistent, and Dani wondered if they might be safer in a church than in a store anyway.

When they arrived at the church door, however, it would not yield to Dani's tug.

Oleksiy, who seemed to understand the meaning of a locked door well enough, looked disappointed. He stared upward with big eyes, as if the church had meant more to him than simple refuge. Dani turned away, shepherding the children toward the sidewalk, when she heard the door behind her rattle and open.

"Pardon me, do you need help?"said a man with a soft Ukrainian accent and an even softer smile. He was wearing a black cassock with a white-tabbed collar. Dani did not, as a general rule, trust men of the cloth, but in this moment, she was not in a position to be picky.

"I am sorry to disturb you," Dani said. "But may I borrow your telephone? We are stranded and need to contact my friend."

"But of course. This way."

As soon as they had crossed the threshold into the building, the priest locked the door behind them. Dani felt a brief twinge of concern. But if he tried to keep them from leaving, she could easily shoot through one of the many windows lining the hallway.

"There is a phone in my office. I am Father Lytvy-nenko, by the way," he continued, as he fell into step on Dani's left. The girls stayed close to her other side, while Oleksiy roamed a yard or so away from them, clearly fasci-nated by the statuary, decoration, and architecture.

"Dani," Dani replied to the priest. She did not know the children's real names, so she did not offer them. "Thank you for granting us hospitality. You did not have to."

"On the contrary," Father Lytvynenko said. "Our lord and savior has made it quite clear that those in need, especially children, are to be assisted at every opportunity."

Dani fought a smile, as the Julep in her mind rolled her eyes. Julep trusted the kindness of strangers even less than Dani did.

"Are you sure that a phone is all you require?" the priest asked. "No offense meant, but you look like you could use food, rest, and perhaps even some medical attention?"

Dani assessed her various wounds and noticed a slight dampness on her injured arm that she had not noticed in the midst of the mission. She looked down to see a trickle of blood running onto her hand from under her jacket sleeve. She pulled the cuff lower and raised her arm across her abdomen, hoping the pressure from her sleeve would help seal the wound. It must have broken open when they were crashing through the forest brush. Petrov would be annoyed. He liked her to heal completely between her training sessions.

"The use of your phone will be enough. Thank you."

When they arrived at the priest's office, a janitor in a creased uniform glanced at them sharply before picking up the office trash bin and ducking out of the room. The children helped themselves to a glass jar holding color-fully wrapped candies.

Dani spotted a black phone on a heavy oak desk in the center of the room. She gravitated to it at once, lifting the receiver to her ear and dialing Han's number from memory. On the other end, the phone rang repeatedly before sending her through to Han's voicemail.

This better be good. BEEP.

Dani heaved a disappointed sigh into the handset.

"Han. There was a..." Dani flicked a surreptitious look at the priest, who had taken a seat in an armchair in the corner opposite the desk and opened a book. "...complication...with the drop off. I need you to call me at..." Then she read the number written on the label affixed to the base of the phone and hung up the receiver.

She hovered there for a minute, hands on the desk, blood dripping onto the blotter, while she tried to think of what to do next.

Her thoughts turned inevitably to Julep. What would Julep do in this situation? She would marshal her resources. She would bring in her crew. She would call Dani. But Dani did not have a crew. She did not even have Han.

The compulsion to find Julep in that moment was strong. Dani could take the children to her, turn them over to Mike Ramirez to keep them safe from whatever was chasing them.

But almost as soon as she entertained the thought, she dismissed it. The FBI could easily be bound by law to return them to their pursuers. Dani simply did not know enough to give them to anyone.

She noticed a closed laptop laying on top of a small bookshelf along the far wall of the office under a window.

"May I borrow your computer?" she asked. When the priest raised his eyes at her in question, she clarified, "I would like to check the news, if I may."

The priest rose to his feet, set his book aside, and retrieved the laptop from the bookshelf. He typed in a password, which Dani did not observe, and opened a browser window. He handed her the laptop, but the disquiet in his expression betrayed his concern. He did not ask her for her story, and she would not know what to tell him if he did. The sooner they were out of the church, the better for him.

She thanked the priest, then sat on a stool under the window, the laptop propped awkwardly on her knee. She typed the words *missing children*. She could speak English well enough after the years she had spent serving Petrov, and he had taught her to read it as well. But she still felt like she was filtering her thoughts through several layers of cheesecloth when she had to translate from Ukrainian to English, and then from spoken English to written.

Her initial search returned far too many results to be useful, so she added *Chicago today* to the search bar. Nothing relevant displayed on the first three pages. Then she searched *airport Chicago arrest today*. Finally, something useful surfaced. An article on ABC7 Eyewitness News reported a man in a turban had been arrested after a disturbance near the O'Hare airport. The article had very little information, but it appeared the man had been alone when arrested by the Chicago police, and that he had somehow been responsible for significant damage to some expensive aeronautical equipment.

Dani breathed a sigh of relief. At least Karanveer had not been captured by whoever was chasing the children. Or worse, killed. Being arrested might make life difficult for a while, but he would likely remain unhurt. Still, that did not reveal what exactly the children were running from or a location Dani could take them where they might be safe.

As Dani searched for information, the children started to actually talk to each other, as they tried the various candies in the dish. Nadia sorted them into rows of matching colors, while Oleksiy folded the empty wrappers into the tiniest squares imaginable and arranged them in patterns on the table.

The priest watched them with a soft smile from the chair in which he was pretending to read his book. Tatyana noticed him and brought him a piece of candy, handing it to him with a few words Dani doubted the priest understood. He took the candy graciously, though, saying thank you in Ukrainian. Tatyana, clearly pleased, wandered back to her siblings.

Returning to her search, Dani typed *missing Uyghur children October*, and pressed ENTER.

Children of Exiled Uyghur Political Leader Detained in XUAR

Two nieces and a nephew of exiled Uyghur freedom fighter Yusup Dolkun have been detained and sent to a state-run boarding school in the Xinjiang Uyghur Autonomous Region (XUAR). Their father, Adil Dolkun, was forced to return to Iran without his wife, Meryem, or children. The whereabouts of Meryem Dolkun are still unknown. Political operatives familiar with the Uyghur humanitarian crisis in China speculate that the detainment of the children was intentionally targeted at Yusup Dolkun to curb his diplomatic efforts at ending the imprisonment and forced labor of the Uyghur people.

Dani leaned back against the window casement, ignoring the pain it caused her arm as she turned this possibility over in her mind. The story fit their circumstances. And it would explain the operatives at the airport hangar. The people responsible for the capture of children as politically valuable as those mentioned in the article would not give them up easily. Not when their custody provided leverage over a man perceived to be an enemy of the state.

Dani wondered how much Han knew. She clearly knew something, even if she felt she could not tell Dani. And it raised another possibility. Perhaps the reason Han was not returning her call was because the children had been traced to her first.

Dani closed the browser window and shut the laptop.

She needed Julep. Dani's skills were limited to those needed for intimidation and protection. She was not a tactician. She had no idea what to do next beyond lay low. But no amount of laying low would convince their pursuers to give up the hunt. And by now, if they indeed had taken Han, then Dani had to assume they knew that she had the children. Which meant it was only a matter of time before they would turn every Ukrainian establishment in the Chicago area on its ear to find them.

She pushed herself off the stool and set the laptop back on the file cabinet. Plan or no plan, they needed to move on. But before she could say as much to their host, the door to the priest's office burst inward, trapping the priest behind it.

6

THE CONSULATE

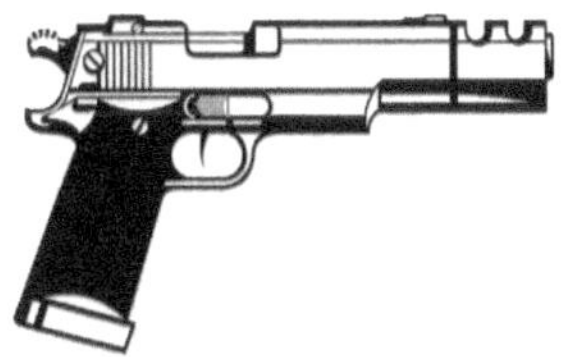

The children scrambled to the far side of the file cabinet, away from the doorway, which was now full of men. But these were not the operatives from the airport. These men Dani knew. The one standing in front, she knew almost better than she knew herself.

"Cowering in a church, my dear?" Petrov sneered. "If you were trying to run, this is an ineffective way to go about it."

The children scuttled behind Dani, unfortunately calling attention to themselves. Had they stayed behind the file cabinet, they might have evaded Petrov's notice.

"Report," he barked harshly at her.

"I was not trying to run," Dani said. "I am doing a favor for a friend. I would have already returned by now, but I ran into a few obstacles."

The priest made to push out from behind the door, but Dani shot him a quick look, which she hoped he interpreted as *stay put*. Petrov was unstable at the best of times, with no moral compunctions about eliminating loose ends, even if they were relatively innocuous.

"That wasn't part of our deal, I'm afraid," Petrov said with deceptive mildness as he oozed into the room. "No contact with the grifter. We agreed there would be consequences."

"Not that friend," Dani said through clenched teeth. "You know I would not risk her. This friend is an enforcer —a colleague."

Petrov glided forward and, with gloved fingers, took Nadia's chin in his hand. It was a mark of her trauma that she did not react. The blank expression, which had just begun to fade, returned in an instant. She stared at the wall as if seeing nothing.

"A bit too young for the program," Petrov commented.

'The program' he referred to was the trafficking business that Dani and Julep had obliterated the previous year. As far as Dani knew, Petrov had not restarted it. It would be foolish of him to try, given the amount of scrutiny he and his enterprises were under.

He was more likely trying to get under Dani's skin, nettle her into revealing how invested she was in the children. But Dani refused to play this game. Hiding her true motivations would only weaken her and waste time.

"You already know who they are," Dani said.

Petrov nodded, smirking at her frankness.

"So what do you intend to do with them?"

Petrov's smirk remained, but the expression behind his eyes soured. He had wanted her to bite, to beg, to try to escape. But she had never once given him that satisfaction, and she would not start now.

"I do not intend to do anything with them," he said, stepping back and signaling to two of his men. "But I have *colleagues* who would like a word with them. And since we are in the mode of doing favors for friends, I imagine we can give the children a ride as far as, say, the Chinese Consulate?"

A chill ran down Dani's spine. The consulate was sovereign soil and well protected. Once inside the building, it would be nearly impossible to get the children out again. Even more so with Petrov watching her every move. But she had no choice. She could not act against Petrov directly without compromising the safety of the children and the priest.

Petrov held out a hand expectantly, waiting for her to comply with his unvoiced command. She capitulated, unholstering her gun and laying it flat, grip first, in the palm of his hand. He pocketed the weapon and left the room. Dani followed him out like a trained dog.

Once they were all out in the hallway, Dani noticed the janitor from earlier. He looked both nervous and self-satisfied, which meant that he had probably informed on them for a reward.

She pitied the man his foolishness, but she did not intervene when Petrov shot him. She merely shielded the children from seeing him crumple to the blood-speckled carpet. She hoped the priest remained hidden until they were gone.

The journey to the consulate was both agonizingly long and far too brief. Dani doubted she would have an opportunity to get the children away from Petrov before arriving at the consulate building. Her one consolation was that probably the government itself would not be directly involved in the recapture of the Uyghur children in U.S. territory. More than likely, contractors had been hired for the job to avoid risking diplomatic relations. Dani was not equipped to fight government operatives on her own, but contractor operatives were another story. Contractors lacked context and conviction, which often led them to make mistakes.

Tatyana burrowed into Dani's side the moment they climbed into the backseat of the Range Rover. She was shivering, so Dani draped her leather jacket over the girl. Dani's arm was still bleeding. Oleksiy saw it and handed her a wadded tissue from his pocket. Dani took it with a nod of thanks and pressed it to her cut. Nadia stared through the window as if none of them existed.

The SUV rolled to a stop at the curb outside of the consulate's side entrance. The building was a massive, rectangular box with square mirrors in neat rows on all sides. Dani was unsurprised that they had not been invited to the main door.

The roll-up garage gate opened, and the driver pulled the car into the underground parking lot. Petrov's crew, Dani, and the children climbed out of the SUV into the garage. Thirteen operatives in now familiar black paramilitary uniforms met them at the elevators. Close up, Dani could make out a silver sigil she did not recognize on their sleeves.

The guards escorted them to a lecture auditorium with quality utility carpeting and a front wall made of whiteboard. From inside the building, the mirrors became tinted glass. Dani glanced at the traffic on the streets below as she searched the room for exit options. Nothing helpful jumped out at her immediately, but conditions were continually changing. For now, two paramilitary goons with rifles guarded each door.

A side door opened, permitting a man in an expensive, blue business suit with a floral pocket square and ascot into the room. He looked relaxed and genial enough, the hands in his pockets rucking up the unbuttoned panels of his suit jacket. Dani did not trust his informal posturing, of course. The most brightly colored snakes were usually the most poisonous.

"Welcome to the Consulate General of the People's Republic of China in Chicago. My name is Li. I will be seeing to your needs while we wait for the transportation team to arrive."

"The children need food," Dani said, partly because it was true, and partly because the more intersections she could make between their prison and the routes to the outside world, the more likely an escape opportunity would emerge.

Li gestured to one of the assistants who had come in with him. She nodded and left.

Petrov leaned against the podium on the sunken stage and regarded Li. "I imagine you are relieved to have your charges returned."

Li smiled in acknowledgement. "We are. And I imagine you have a request for us that might make your trouble worthwhile."

"As it happens, I do. A mere trifle for someone with the political reach of the Consul."

"You have but to ask," Li said, gesturing as if offering Petrov a well stocked buffet.

"If the Consul would be so kind, I would very much like to meet with the Minister of Energy on a matter of infrastructure."

Dani took care to show no outward sign of surprise. Why would a Ukrainian mob boss want to meet with the energy secretary of China? Or any energy secretary, for that matter?

"I will relay your request to the Consul," Li said. Then he and his associates left, and the guards drifted into their places barring the door.

"It appears I must thank you, my dear," Petrov said to

Dani. Under the expensive cologne he wore, he still smelled of lye, proving that no matter how richly he dressed, he would always be сміття from the slums of Kharkiv.

"Whatever I did, I guarantee it was not for you."

"Regardless, I am grateful for the opportunity, however unintentional it may have been on your part."

"Why does the Republic want them so badly?"

"I hardly keep track of these petty political affairs, but the rumor is that the children are close relatives of a known Uyghur terrorist. They likely plan to use the children as an incentive to stop his influence in the region."

"Is he a terrorist? Or a freedom fighter?"

Petrov sighed as if disappointed and shook his head. "Frankly, Danijela. I am surprised that you would involve yourself in another altruistic scheme so soon after your last one turned deadly."

"I did not kill anyone," she said.

Petrov rubbed his chest where she had shot him that night. "Not for lack of trying."

"If I had been trying to kill you," she said plainly, "you would be dead."

"True enough," he acknowledged. "It is the grifter who has turned you from a cold-blooded killer, then. She has dulled your edge to near uselessness."

Dani was still a killer. Always would be, because she had killed. It was being a killer that had broken her, not Julep. Julep had offered her friendship in spite of it. Had tried to offer her a path to redemption, not that Dani could ever walk it. But Julep had tried, and that meant a lot.

"Do you not see yourself in them?" Dani asked Petrov, truly curious. Compassion was not possible for him, that much she knew. But recognition? She was not certain.

"Of course, I do," Petrov said, his smirk sinking into disgust. "But no one helped *me*. I clawed my fortune out of the pitiless bedrock of this world with my own bleeding hands. Look at them. Half your age, and yet they know reality better than you do. Why do you continue to resist? Especially when you are constantly being punished for it?"

Dani did not respond. She may not know better than to get involved when someone asked for aid, but she did know when answering Petrov would be a mistake.

Li returned then, notably lacking his associates. Instead, he had brought with him several dining staff and three carts of food for the children. Tatyana and Oleksiy looked at Dani first before moving toward the carts. Dani nodded permission. Oleksiy plucked at Nadia's sleeve, and she shuffled with them to the nearest cart. A young server, a woman with black hair piled high on her head the way Julep's sometimes was, kneeled down, smiling at Tatyana and handing her a pastry. Tatyana took it, her expression grave and suspicious, but she ate it.

"Mr. Petrov," Li said. "Your request has been granted. If you and your team would please follow me."

Petrov leveled a look at Dani that made it clear she was expected to accompany him. She hated leaving the children, but she could not disable a trap that she did not know the workings of.

When she moved toward the door, Tatyana made a noise of distress and ran to her, catching her hand as if she meant to accompany them. Dani would have let her come had not the guard nearest them tightened his grip on his rifle.

Dani kneeled next to the girl, pulling her phone out of her pocket and handing it to her. The screen was still black and lifeless, but she hoped the message would translate.

I will come back for you.

The girl took the phone and tucked it to her chest with a resigned sigh and let go of Dani's hand.

Dani stood, a weight like iron on her chest. It was a hard thing, turning her back on the children to follow Petrov from the room.

The maze of carpeted hallways and closed black doors did little to improve Dani's chances of rescuing the children. She needed more time to find an exit route, but time was one of many things she did not have. There was no guarantee the children would even still be there after Petrov concluded his business with the energy secretary. Li had not said when their transportation would arrive.

They reached a nexus point of several interconnected hallways. A column of elevators served as the center of the hub. Li pushed the button to call one of the cars to their floor.

As they waited, Dani scanned the adjacent hallways as much as she could from her position, looking for anything she could use as leverage to help her and the children escape. As luck would have it, one of the doors in the next hallway over had been left ajar. She took a surreptitious step back, slowly so as not to draw attention, and craned her neck to see if there might be something of use. But an unguarded doorway to freedom was not what she found. Instead, sitting in a chair, head bent low, she saw…

"Han…" Dani breathed involuntarily.

So she had been taken, as Dani suspected. No wonder she had not returned Dani's call. Wrist restraints, mussed hair, and slumped posture…all further evidence that her presence here was not by choice.

Li took notice of Dani's interest in the conference room. He moved to block her view of Han as the elevator dinged its arrival. His expression seemed calculating rather than alarmed, which indicated a high degree of confidence that neither Dani nor Han posed any kind of real threat.

Dani followed Petrov into the elevator. Li was the last on board, and he pushed the topmost button as he turned to face the doors.

"The Consul is a very busy man," he said. "You will have twenty minutes."

"That should be sufficient," Petrov said, his tone

clipped. He clearly did not like Li, but then he rarely cared for anyone he considered an underling.

The elevator dinged again, and the doors swished open with a puff of ventilated air. Dani followed Li into an opulent sitting room with floor-to-ceiling mirrored panels interspersed with art-covered walls. The mirrored panels served as reflectors of light from the display cases of ancient artifacts set on pedestals in front of them. The effect was a museum-like quality—as if many more pedestals of artifacts were present than actually were.

Arrangements of plushly upholstered furniture were set attractively in self-contained pockets around the room, though no one was seated in them. A fully stocked bar lined the wall to the left of the elevator. The far wall of the room consisted of the same one-way windows from the lecture room several floors below.

As Li led them to the nearest sitting area, Dani broke off from the group and walked toward the windows. She looked down to determine where the street-level exits were on this side of the building. A window-washer platform a couple of floors above the one they had just come from blocked her view to the south toward Ontario Street. It appeared as if all the exits on this side were through retail shops.

A small, sleek helicopter approached from the direction Dani was looking. It rose as it flew past the room's bank of windows, only its skids visible at their level.

"Apologies for the noise," Li said, looking more smug

than apologetic. "Our partnership with Vertiport allows us to operate one of only three helipads in downtown Chicago..."

Dani tuned out any further explanation, plotting her next move.

She had just found her exit strategy.

7

THE ROOF

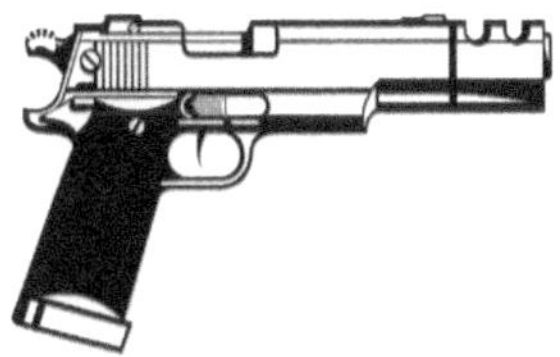

Li left to notify the Consul of their arrival, and Dani took the opportunity to survey the room. She found nothing she could use as a weapon, and only one door aside from the elevator leading out of the Consul's suite.

She did stumble across one helpful item—a scale model of the consulate building displaying the helipad. It showed a cross-section of the building, the route to the roof helpfully marked with red arrows. She studied the layout of the floor she suspected she had come from as well, trying to identify the conference room where she had seen Han.

Petrov wandered over to her. She ignored him as he closed the distance.

"I would not test the patience of these people,

підручний. I doubt they would be as forgiving of your idiosyncrasies as I am. They do not have the benefit of our long-standing history."

"No, they do not," Dani observed quietly. They would underestimate her as Petrov would not.

The door that separated the sitting room from the Consul's inner sanctum opened, and Li emerged. "The Consul will see you now."

Petrov nodded and approached the door. When Andriy and Yakiv stood up to follow him, he stopped, a flicker of what looked like curiosity crossing his face. He signaled them to wait rather than follow. They seemed nonplussed by the unusual order but obeyed and returned to their seats.

Li led Petrov through the door, and it fell closed behind them.

Dani wandered back toward the bar as if continuing to explore the room. But when she reached it, she leaned over the polished wood, pretending to examine the liquor collection. She grabbed a bottle of something brown and pulled it out from under the counter. When she cleared the top of the bar, she purposefully fumbled the bottle and dropped it. The bottle cracked on the foot rail of the bar, splashing amber liquid across the white carpet.

"My apologies!" she said to one of the guards, hoping he would read her awkwardness as embarrassment rather than the effect of her being a terrible liar. "Is there a bathroom where I can find towels?"

He pointed to the exit in the mirror-paneled wall. "Left, two doors."

Dani preempted Andriy's objection as she hurried to the door. "Could you help him? I will get towels."

Then she passed through the mirrored door without a backward glance. She turned left as directed by the guard to reduce suspicion. But as soon as the door clicked shut behind her, she turned and ran flat out in the opposite direction, through the empty corridor and toward the closest stairwell. She had limited time before they followed her, or worse, notified the children's guards.

She skidded to slow her momentum, then crashed through the stairwell door. She leaped down three stairs at a time, hands sliding along the cool railings for balance. Two levels lower, she seized the opportunity of another consulate worker entering the stairwell to fly through the door without a passkey.

She had dropped two levels, not far enough to reach the children. But the building was a giant cube. She could still make progress before heading downward again.

This level was more heavily populated, making it impossible for Dani to avoid detection. She weaved through the foot traffic, knocking into people when she could not avoid them. She would sooner shove an aide out a window than slow down.

Finally, she arrived at another bank of elevators. She punched every button for every elevator in the bank. When the first one opened, she jumped in and pushed the button for every floor. Then she jumped out again and got into the next, repeating the action. When the final elevator arrived, she hopped in and pushed the button for the floor she hoped the children were on as well as every button lower. If security was tracking her movements, that would delay them.

Dani paced the elevator, breathing hard, feeling like a caged tiger as the car took her closer to her target. She could not avoid the guards forever. By now her absence would have been noted, the alarm raised, and they would know from her race across the tenth floor approximately where she was. Dani was going to need a weapon soon.

When the elevator doors slid open, Dani dropped instinctively to her knees, narrowly avoiding the muzzle of an AM-17 compact assault rifle. She aimed a pointed kick at the security guard's lateral knee joint. He cried out as he collapsed, his kneecap dislocated. Dani scooped up the rifle as she rolled out of the elevator and across to the opposite wall, coming out of the roll with the weapon aimed and sweeping the room. No other security guards were in sight.

She scuttled back to the downed security guard. Patting his utility pockets, she found a Magnum and some extra ammunition. She dragged the man into a darkened office and shut him in with the door locked. She could afford to be more circumspect, now that she was so close to the children. Another hallway to the left, a corridor more from there, and she should be at the lecture room.

This floor was either far less populated than the tenth, or an announcement had been made that a dangerous criminal was on the loose, and the consulate staff had better shelter in place. Dani would place a bet on the latter.

She turned left, then right again, lifting the rifle to her shoulder as she approached the familiar double doors of the lecture room. She listened at the crack for a moment but heard no sounds within. Heart pounding, she threw open the doors to find the room empty.

She staggered back, dismayed and near panic at first. But upon further inspection, the room was not entirely empty. The young woman who had served the children food had ducked down between the rows, her kind smile now replaced with a look of terror.

"Where did they go?" Dani demanded. "If you care about their fate, tell me."

The woman pressed her hands together to stop them from shaking. "Th-the roof," she whispered. "Th-the…"

Dani swore, her throat like gravel. "The helicopter."

Of course the transport team's plan to extract the children was the same as Dani's. It was a good plan.

Dani doubled back at once, retracing her steps at a run. She would have to free Han first now and pray that they could make it all the way through the building a second time without getting caught.

But when Dani reached the hub point with the hallway that branched off to where Han was being held, what was left of Dani's luck had run out. She barely had time to register the eight or so guards blocking the door to Han's conference room and duck behind the safety of the wall before they opened fire.

Dani returned fire, pointing her pistol at the overhead lights above the guards. Cursing and shouting burst from the hallway as the guards took cover from the shrapnel.

While they were distracted, Dani rushed them, using her gun as a battering ram. She pushed three guards to the floor and whirled to hit another hard in the jaw. As he fell back, another two rushed in to fill the gap. She shouldered her weapon and shot one guard in the arm, then pivoted to do the same with the second. Before she could pull the trigger, though, he threw his hands up in the air, signaling surrender. Without hesitation, she flipped the barrel end around and pistol whipped him across the temple.

Then she spun and kicked open the flimsy conference-room door. Three men guarded a bound and gagged Han. One stood just to the left of the door, while two others gripped Han's arms on either side. The two holding Han carried guns similar in size and firepower to Dani's—and neither of them were pointing their weapon at Han's head. Contractors. Maybe Dani's luck had held after all.

"Падати!" Dani commanded.

Han obediently sagged to the floor, boneless, forcing her captors to focus their attention on bolstering her weight.

With Han's two operatives distracted, Dani tossed her AM-17 to the third man in the room. He instinctively dropped his own weapon to catch hers. And by the time he had recovered, she was on him, hitting him at the base of his skull with a two-handed grip around the pistol. He sank to the ground as bonelessly as Han had.

Dani recovered the AM-17 and holstered his handgun under her jacket. She tucked the handgun she had knocked him out with in her waistband. Meanwhile, Han had taken her fight to the floor. She had laced both legs around the soldier who had been on her left, immobilizing his weapon arm and carefully keeping him between herself and the second captor.

Dani grabbed the second man from behind, locking his arm behind him and wrenching his shoulder out of joint. As he howled in agony, she used his injured arm as leverage, spinning him around and out the door she had burst through. She slammed the door closed again, barricading it as best she could with the body of the guard she had knocked unconscious.

"Hurry, Han," Dani barked, as she scanned the room for other doors. There were none.

She climbed onto the conference room table just as Han managed to flip her opponent to the floor. She clamped her still bound arms around his neck, cutting off just enough of his oxygen to put him to sleep. Then she dropped him, took the gag from her mouth, and fished around in his pocket for keys to her restraints.

Shouts sounded in the hallway. Too close. There was not enough left of a door to shield them for long, and Dani very much doubted that the contractors cared enough about each other to be squeamish about accidentally shooting their unconscious compatriots.

"We do not have time, Han! You can run with bound hands."

Han cursed in her three favorite languages, as she joined Dani on the table. Dani cupped her hands, and Han stepped into them, leaning her wrists against Dani's shoulder.

"One, two..."

Dani hoisted her up high enough for her to pop through a ceiling tile and into the liminal space between the drop-ceiling and the floor above it. Once Han had found a strut strong enough to hold their weight, she reached back for Dani. Dani jumped high enough to grab hold of Han's wrists. Han grunted and swore but managed to help Dani scramble up.

Dani laid the ceiling tile back in place. Then they crawled as quickly as they could along the load-bearing struts and larger pipes.

"The children?" Han asked, voice hoarse with effort. She looked the worse for wear, cuts on her face and what looked like bruising starting around her neck. Dani imagined under her clothes probably looked worse.

"Roof," Dani replied, panting. "Extraction by helicopter."

Han hissed instead of swearing this time, likely to save breath and energy for the journey, which she had to somehow manage with her hands cuffed.

Dani led them in a stair-step diagonal direction away from the core of the building.

"Where are we going?" Han asked after several minutes of clambering over ductwork and cable trays, and fighting through thick electrical wiring.

"Windows," Dani said. "Only way to roof."

"Can't climb the side of a building with tied hands."

Dani ignored her protest. They were close.

She paused for a moment to listen but heard no sound coming from below. So she removed the nearest ceiling tile to find an empty office below them. Dani set the tile down again and inched a few feet further on to position them over a heavy oak desk. She removed that ceiling tile and looked down. The desk itself was clear of everything but a few small picture frames.

She lowered herself down awkwardly and dropped the remaining meter or so to the desk. Then she helped Han down as well. As they climbed off the desk, Dani jogged to the window and looked out, her chest lightening with relief to find the window washers on their platform, blissfully unaware of anything going on inside the building.

They looked to be a few offices further to the south, so Dani hustled Han out through their office door into an offshoot corridor with no one in sight.

"You can't be serious," Han said.

"You will not have to climb," Dani noted, as she made a sharp right into an employee lunch room. The window washers were right outside, but they took no notice of Han and Dani. The one-way glass seemed to prevent them from seeing in at all.

Dani led Han to a nearby table.

"Loop the handcuff chain over the corner."

Without questioning, Han did so. Dani pulled the handgun out of her holster, aimed it at the chain between the bracelets, and fired a single shot. Shards of formica ricocheted from the table-top, scratching Dani's cheek.

"Fuck!" Han cried out cradling her wrist. "That fucking hurt."

"Are you okay?" Dani asked, helping her to her feet.

"I'll live," she said, glaring at Dani and rubbing her wrist where the manacle still dangled like a bracelet. But she took the handgun Dani handed her without further complaint.

Dani faced the window, positioning herself equidistant between the two men. The washers were at either end of the platform, and the platform itself was wide enough that they should be relatively safe from—

"Dani! You can't—"

Dani pulled the trigger. The tempered glass shattered in a spiderweb pattern, a spray of shards shooting outward along the path of the bullet. Then the rest of the window collapsed downward in an avalanche of tinkling destruction.

Each man instinctively ducked, covering his head. The small, balding one recovered from the surprise first.

"What the—?"

"Unhook your restraints and get off the platform," Dani commanded, pointing her gun at him. "Both of you. Now."

With shaking fingers, the men complied, the bald one glaring at her. When both men were safely inside the building, Dani and Han climbed out onto the platform.

"You better know what you're doing," Han said, worried.

Dani punched the controls to elevate the platform back to the roof. If she and Han did not make it to the roof in the next few minutes, the children would be gone.

Dani took the opportunity to check her magazine—just over half full. She replaced it with the extra she had stolen from the first guard.

"What's the plan, Ivanov?" Han asked. "Even if we manage to recover the children, we won't make it to street level."

"No need," Dani said. "We will use the helicopter."

"Helicopter?" Han stared at Dani as if she had suggested sprouting wings. "And just who do you think is going to pilot it?"

"You flew helicopters for the military."

"I flew *a* helicopter for the military. They're not all the same!"

"Then you will take the current pilot hostage. You will at least know if they try to sabotage the flight."

Han shook her head in disbelief. But as the platform leveled with the roof, she crouched defensively and raised her gun, ready to do what was needed.

Dani hopped from the platform to the roof and darted to the nearest HVAC unit. She could see the helipad from here, but it was on the far north side of the building from their position.

Dani gestured to Han to go first. There were no guards on this side of the building, but it would take mere minutes to reach the edge of the helipad.

They kept near the edge of the roof, sticking close to the wall to avoid detection. When they reached the divider between them and the helipad, Dani directed Han to stop and duck behind the short wall.

"I count seven," Han said. "Where are—?"

Before she could finish the question, four more hired guns with the same insignia on their uniforms, marched the children through the rooftop door onto the helipad. Petrov and his enforcers were nowhere in sight, but that did not surprise Dani. Petrov's business had nothing to do with the children. He was likely below, either looking for Dani or on his way back to the hotel without her.

In any case, Li was present and waiting for the children halfway between the door and the helicopter. When the children were within his reach, Li lunged for Nadia, swooping her into a loose hold and spinning her around toward where Dani and Han were hiding. As he did so, he pulled a gun from under his jacket and aimed it at Nadia's head.

8

———

THE STATION

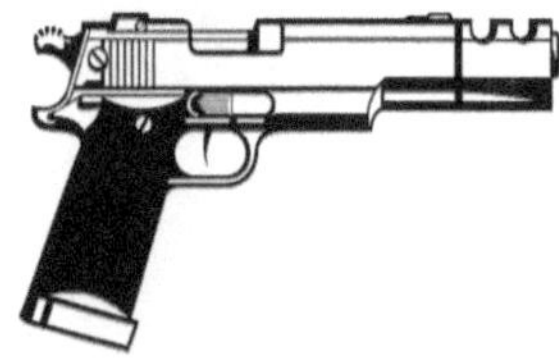

"I know you're there!" Li shrieked. "Come out, or the child dies!"

Li did not appear to know their exact location, as he was addressing the roof as a whole, and his stance was angled forty-five degrees from Dani and Han's position.

"Don't do it," Han hissed. "The second you pop up, they'll kill you."

"One child more or less makes no difference to us!" Li continued, yelling over the whirring blades of the helicopter. "Dolkun will only capitulate faster if we prove we are willing to follow through on our threats!"

"They will not risk the shot at this distance with the wind shear," Dani answered Han.

Han did not waste her breath arguing, but that did not mean she approved. Regardless, Dani stood as ordered, guns raised above her head in surrender. She would not let Nadia die.

...your story is your best offense...

Julep's voice floated through Dani's mind unbidden, appearing as she often did from the mists of Dani's subconscious when Dani least expected it—and often when she could ill afford it. But in this moment, perhaps phantom-Julep had a point. If Dani could just delay the inevitable long enough, Han could relocate to a more advantageous position.

"I am not here for the children," Dani shouted back. "I only need to retrieve my mobile phone."

"Your what?"

"My phone!" Dani repeated louder, as the wind whipped up around her. "I gave it to the child to pacify her when we left the auditorium. I need it back."

"You expect me to believe that you fought through security, at great risk to your life, over an easily replace-able electronic device?"

The story unfolded in Dani's mind as if Julep herself were telling it. Dani stepped over the short wall to the helipad, drawing closer to Li to move his line of sight even further away from Han.

"As you say, it is an electronic device." Dani drew out her syllables, stalling as long as she could. "It holds data beyond telephone numbers and text messages. Sensitive data. I came to collect it, but the children had already been moved."

"So you gunned down my security officers?"

Dani would have shrugged, but her arms were still raised above her head. "They shot first. I was defending myself."

Li relaxed his hold on Nadia. Then he gestured for the closest guard to approach. The guard obeyed, and Li swiftly conveyed what Dani had said. Or at least, Dani hoped he had. It was difficult to hear more than snatches above the sound of the blades.

The guard nodded and headed toward the other children. Dani held her breath, ready to spring if his gun so much as twitched in Tatyana's direction. Instead, he reached out and grabbed Dani's phone, which Tatyana had been clutching to her chest with her stuffed unicorn.

Tatyana would not give up the phone easily. She clung to it with as much fervor as she did her unicorn. The guard had to sling his rifle over his shoulder to free both hands in order to pry the device from her grip. When he finally succeeded, her unicorn dropped to the ground as well, and the expression on her face was one Dani recognized well from their escape into the sewer.

Tatyana let loose a screech loud enough that it nearly drowned out the whirring of the nearby helicopter. Several of the closest guards winced at the high-pitched screaming. While everyone was distracted by Tatyana, Dani sprung at Li, knocking his gun arm up and away from Nadia. Then Dani tackled him to the tarmac, knocking him unconscious with his own pistol.

She grabbed Nadia's hand while the guards shouted to each other and regrouped. She started to pull Nadia back behind the wall for cover, but Han leaped out from behind the other guards and took three of them down before they even knew someone was there.

Dani switched directions at once and practically dragged Nadia back toward the helicopter. Nadia did not resist, thankfully, but nor did she exactly cooperate. It took longer than Dani would have liked to get her to the helicopter.

The pilot began to climb down from the cockpit, but Dani swung her gun on him at once. He threw up his hands and sank back into his seat, shaking with fear. Civilian, probably. He might still be a liability, though.

She held the gun on him as she waved the other two children over. Tatyana was still weeping hard enough that Dani was afraid she would have to leave the pilot after all. But Oleksiy came to her rescue, scooping up both the unicorn and Dani's phone, which the guard had dropped in his haste to defend himself against Han. The boy handed both items to his sister, which calmed her enough for Oleksiy to lead her toward Dani.

As the children huddled with Nadia in Dani's shadow, Dani swung the rifle in her left hand to shoot a guard aiming his AR-15 at Han. Dani's bullet hit his arm, forcing him to drop his weapon. Han continued her assault on the two remaining guards, swirling around them as if she were smoke, her body solidifying only to kick and disarm and maneuver them so that they neutralized each other.

"Han!" Dani shouted, then turned her attention back to the pilot. "You will take them wherever she tells you. Do you understand?"

The pilot nodded eagerly, sweat pouring down his face.

Dani urged the children into the helicopter, buckling them in as best she could one handed. Han arrived then, her own gun trained on the pilot as she climbed into the co-pilot's seat.

"They're coming!" Han yelled above the engine noise. She pulled headphones over her ears and gestured toward additional sets of headphones hanging under the seats. "I wedged the door shut, but it won't last long! There was no way to lock it from this side!"

Dani placed headphones over each child's ears.

"What are you doing?" Han demanded. "Get in!"

"I am not coming," Dani said.

"Why not?" she yelled, alarmed.

"I have to stall them, keep them from following you. I must run interference, or you will not escape."

"You—!"

But Han stopped herself. She was as skilled in tactical extraction as Dani was, if not more so.

"Fine," she said at last, turning back angrily to buckle herself in and give the pilot directions that Dani could not hear.

Dani pulled back, taking stock of her energy reserves, her opportunities for cover, as the roof door quivered under battering from the other side.

Then Dani felt a light touch on her hand. Tatyana, face tear-streaked and sad, held out Dani's phone. Dani took the phone and looked down at its dark screen.

Another crash against the roof door sounded behind her.

Dani handed the phone back to Tatyana, wrapping her small fingers around its edges.

"Keep it," she said to Tatyana, though she knew Tatyana would not understand the words. "Keep it safe for me."

Then she leaned over and gave Tatyana a light kiss on her forehead.

The roof door burst open behind them, spilling a dozen guards onto the tarmac in less than a second.

"Go!" Dani shouted to Han, as she circled to face the enemy, guns raised.

Behind her the helicopter rose up and out over the city, flying the children away at last. But for Dani, the work had just begun.

She blanketed the air just above the guards with bullets, forcing them to drop for cover. Meanwhile, she dove behind a concrete pylon, keeping up enough fire to focus their attention on her rather than the helicopter. Her ammunition did not last, though, and before long, she was forced to surrender.

They took her to a room with no windows, no ceiling tiles, no furniture, and only one door that locked from the outside.

They asked her predictable questions, most of which she could not answer—they could not pry information from a mind that did not have it, no matter how many times they repeated their inquiries. They were not polite about their demands, and though Dani would not have given them the information they sought had she known it, she was relieved not to have to fight the inevitable compulsion to do so to lessen the pain.

She found herself grateful for Petrov's training sessions, which had conditioned her to withstand most of the less savory methods of intelligence gathering. Bruises and broken ribs healed, after all. Blood would eventually replace itself. They could do her no lasting harm, as long as they knew nothing of Julep.

All things considered, she was worthless to them, and once they figured that out, they would toss her in the garbage like every other useless thing.

She just had to survive until trash day.

"JESUS, DANI."

Dani turned at Han's voice behind her. It had been two weeks since the incident at the consulate, and Dani was fairly certain she looked worse now than she did when she had woken up in the alley behind the consulate building and staggered to an emergency room for treatment.

An announcement echoed through the train station, causing Dani to wince. Her ears were still ringing from the blows to her head. The doctor said it would likely ease with time but that there were no guarantees.

"I am glad you made it," Dani said. "I did not know if you would get my message."

"You look awful."

"I feel worse."

Han bit her lip, looking as if she were about to reach up and touch Dani's face the way she used to. But that was a time before Julep, and Han knew it. There was no *them* anymore.

"Did Petrov rescue you?" she asked.

"No," Dani answered, matter-of-factly. "He said that the consequences fit the crime, and that perhaps I would learn this time that people who could not save themselves were a commodity, not a path to salvation."

"Wow," Han said, dropping into one of the church-like pews in the station hall. "What a delusional asshole."

Dani sat next to her. "You are not wrong," she said as she watched people passing by. She wondered if they saw her as a commodity or a person. Maybe they just saw her as an obstacle to avoid. Or a potential liability. A threat. She would not blame them if they did. She was all of those things.

"Karanveer is out of lock-up," Han said. "Thought you might want to know. And I took a detour past St. Joseph's. The priest was relieved to hear that the children were all right and had made it to their destination. He wanted me to give you this."

Han handed her a piece of candy in a bright purple wrapper. A lump formed in Dani's throat, making it difficult for her to swallow. She put the candy in her pocket.

"I made sure the young one had a charging cable for the phone you gave her," Han continued. "Though I don't understand the significance. Why give it to her? Why did she freak out when they tried to take it?"

Dani shrugged. "I cannot explain it. But I am grateful that you did that."

"It was the least I could do, after..."

She cleared her throat, letting the sentence go unfinished.

"And Li?"

"The Consul and the Republic were forced to disavow him and deny all involvement in the detainment and pursuit of the children. Too much negative press on the international stage, or something."

"How are they?" Dani asked, wanting to know more than whether they were all right. Wanting to know that Tatyana still had her unicorn. That Oleksiy had found a beautiful church to explore. That Nadia had not retreated so deep into her shell that she could not come out again.

"I wish I could say that they are home and safe with

their family," Han said. "But they are still on that journey. And even once they get there, they'll still have to recover from all the damage…"

Dani fought the urge to find them, to verify with her own eyes that they were protected. It was not her fight anymore.

"They *are* strangely better, though," Han continued. "Before they met you, they were…unreachable. Even when we spoke to them in Putonghua, their responses were one or two words at most. But their shield cracked during those twenty-four hours with you. Especially the youngest. She is a chatterbox now."

"And Nadia?"

"Nadia?" Han asked, confused.

"Sorry, the oldest girl. I gave them names in my head," Dani explained sheepishly.

Han smirked at her, but there was a fondness in it that seemed uncomplicated by pain. Maybe more had been healed than just the children.

"She is still troubled, of course. All of them are. But the boy takes good care of his sisters."

Dani's heart lightened at the thought of them happy and secure. Even her bruises felt less angry.

"Where are you off to now?" Han asked as another announcement rippled through the cavernous room.

"I do not know," Dani said. "Petrov does not share that information with me."

"Do you know when you'll be back?"

"I do not even know *if* I will be back."

Han looked away, then down, and sniffed. She always hated showing emotion, even to someone she trusted.

"What's your new phone number?" Han asked.

"I do not have a phone."

"Why not?" Han said sharply.

"Petrov says they are a distraction from the work."

"You are not allowed a phone?"

"I am not allowed a lot of things."

"How much longer is this going to go on, Dani? He can't keep you prisoner forever."

"He has not yet broken his promise, or tried to cross a line that I will not allow him to cross."

Han's sharp brows angled down like a falcon diving for prey. "You and your ridiculous honor. You do not owe him this just because you promised him something stupid when you needed information."

"I stay with him for my own reasons, Han."

She sighed in a way that meant she was exasperated and wanted Dani to know it.

The announcer finally called Dani's train, so she stood, gingerly, leaning on the bench for support.

"Wait. How am I supposed to get a hold of you?" Han asked, jumping to her feet as well.

"I will text you a number when I finally manage to acquire a phone," Dani said tiredly. "Take care, Han." Then she set herself on the shortest trajectory toward the train.

"Wait," Han said again, putting herself in front of Dani. "I owe *you* one now. A big one."

She seemed expectant, as if she wanted Dani to call in her debt now. And there was something Dani wanted. Something that needed Han's skillset. Something that had been weighing on her for a long time.

"Keep her safe," Dani said softly. "Keep her safe for me."

The color drained from Han's face, but she did not blink or waver. She did not ask which 'she' Dani meant. She held Dani's gaze and nodded once in acknowledgement. It was enough.

Dani walked through the rotunda to the train platform and did not look back.

One month later

9

THE JUNKYARD

In retrospect, meeting an Albanian mob enforcer nicknamed "Meat Grinder" in a junkyard on the outskirts of Chi-town was perhaps not the wisest decision I've ever made. For one thing, it's well after nightfall, and this junkyard has all the lighting of an underwater cave. For another thing, the Albanians make the Ukrainians I tangled with a year ago look like butterfly collectors. Albanians are notoriously clannish, hypersensitive to insult, and far too trigger-happy for my taste. The Capja syndicate in particular, which is, unluckily for me, the one I happen to be dealing with, has a particularly unsavory reputation. In other words, they're less like a company and more like a powder keg. Even other crime syndicates are hesitant to deal with them.

I pick my way through the weed-choked berms of scrap metal, charting the route back to the main road in my head. The last thing I need is to get lost in here. The broken, rusting corpses hulking in the junkyard shadows remind me of the drowned Chevelle, and, by extension, Dani. I almost lost her with the Chevelle. Then I lost her for real when the Ukrainian mob stole her away from me. Which brings me back to my clandestine meeting with the Meat Grinder. He's going to help me steal her back.

A man's voice growls in the darkness. I don't speak Albanian, but I recognize a command when I hear one. I stop in my tracks.

"I'm Julep Dupree," I say. "I'm here for a meeting."

Another string of unintelligible words snakes out of the darkness. Murphy Donovan, my communications tech specialist, said this was a bad idea. I'm starting to think he was right. Then one word I recognize floats above the rest, and I seize it.

"Yes! That's me. I'm the grifter."

Grifter. I almost snort at the lie. Some grifter I turned out to be. Time and again I've been fooled by enemies right under my nose. I trust all the wrong people and put all the people I love in danger because of it. No grifter worth the name would be so careless. No grifter worth the name would let herself love someone.

Besides, I haven't worked a job since Dani left. With every passing month that there's no word of her whereabouts or her condition, the pressure in my head gets tighter. Another day or two without her and my skull will start to crack.

Even if I could make myself work, my notoriety after the NWI case has taken longer to cool down than I'd like. Mike's mostly kept the paparazzi off my six, but I still get recognized on the street from time to time. It's embarrassing, as well as inconvenient, from a professional perspective. It'll blow over eventually, but for both reasons, I've left Murphy and the rest of the team to keep J.D. & Associates alive.

Meanwhile, Sam, my genius hacker and best friend, is doing everything in his power to help me find Dani, when he isn't trying to decode the data we accessed on the blue-fairy flash drive we recovered during the NWI job last summer. But Petrov, the slimy Ukrainian kingpin who took her, is keeping himself and Dani both so completely off-grid that even Sam can't pick up the trail. Hence, Meat Grinder.

Then he steps out into the mediocre light. I look up and up and up until I finally see his face hovering somewhere around seven feet. This guy is like a monolith with tree trunks for limbs. And he's older than I thought he'd be, balding and puffy around the eyes. I guess I'm used to thinking of Dani when I think *enforcer*. But most enforcers aren't nineteen-year-old girls.

"You look for Petrov, yes?" he grumbles. His enunciation is crap, so it takes me a half-second to figure out what he's saying.

"Yes. Do you know where he is?"

He stands silent for several long minutes, no doubt

trying to translate what I said. There's a reason he's not called The Professor. Actually, there are probably several reasons he's not called The Professor.

"My boss ask why."

Why indeed. Why have I neglected every other relationship and responsibility in my life for the last three months to pursue this futile mission? Why have I lost all interest in everything I ever used to care about? Why have I completely dropped the search for my mother? Why have I all but stopped visiting my father in prison? It's simple really. Because nothing else matters until she's safe.

"He has something I want."

Meat—I think we've bonded enough now to be on a first-name basis—thinks over what I've said for another interminable length of time. Then he grunts some kind of affirmative. He must be wearing an earpiece with a direct line to his boss. Huh. What a great idea. I make a mental note for the next time I'm meeting a homicidal psychopath in an abandoned junkyard. Then I discard the mental note. I'm terrible at remembering backup. At least I let Murphy know where I am and who I'm meeting. That's progress, believe it or not.

"What you are willing to pay?"

I take a deep breath. This is the part I'm dreading. After squaring all my hospital debt from the NWI fiasco four months ago, I don't have the kind of money that would buy me any kind of favors from the Albanians. So I have to trade info for info. Which means someone's likely going to die for me. Again.

"First, I need confirmation that you know where Petrov is."

I wait while Invisible Bossman relays his answer to Meat. The night breeze is still somewhat bearable, despite the onslaught of fall, and I have nowhere else to be right now. Lily will cover for me if our foster mom Angela decides to check on me.

"How we can give you confirmation without location?" he asks dutifully.

"A picture of him taken today would work."

After another minute, Meat answers. "We get picture after you tell us what is payment."

I chew my lip, thinking. My feeble conscience is asserting its misgivings at the top of its lungs. Luckily, my conscience is a pasty-faced, sickly sort of thing and is easily smacked down by my desperate heart.

"One of your lackeys is stealing from you, which I know you know. You give me the location, I give you the name and proof."

I hold up a non-blue-fairy flash drive with the intel I'd dug up on poor Hajdari. It wasn't hard finding the weak link in the Albanians—young accountant addicted to prescription narcotics. It was harder finding out which of the families had tabs on Petrov, who somehow wrangled a get-out-of-jail-free card for himself while leaving his associates to rot. All except Dani. I don't know who's working for him now or what he's even doing. But he's back in Chicago. I can *feel* it. Plus Mike, my FBI handler and foster father, has heard rumblings at the Bureau, and they're making him tetchy.

"What's the hold up?" I ask, shifting my weight uncomfortably. I don't like being left alone too long with my own thoughts. "Can you get me a picture or not?"

Meat grunts and pulls a tablet from his cavernous pocket. He swipes at it awkwardly with his thick fingers. Then he faces it toward me. I inch forward enough to make out a blurry man shape that *could* be Petrov. The dimensions seem right. It's hard to tell for sure, because in addition to the blur, he's in the distance and there's a lot going on in the background. It looks like he's at a carnival gone wrong. Lots of colors tumbled together and just, I don't know, *off* somehow. But in the foreground, there's a clear-as-day picture of the *Harvey Herald* with *October 11* beneath the header.

I pull back, apprehensive. Because whether or not the photo's legit, we've come to the crossroads. Do I give up the drug addict? Do I need the picture so badly that I'd ruin a stranger's life? A stranger, by the way, who's done nothing to me?

But the answer is *yes*. Yes, I do need the picture that badly. Sam and I have come nowhere close to finding Petrov and Dani before tonight. We've tried. For four agonizing months. Months that Petrov could have spent torturing Dani, or even killing her. He could be hurting her right now.

Just the thought of the possibility is untenable. I can't function with her in trouble, and I can't keep not functioning. I have to get her back. Even if it means the drug addict goes down for it. But when I open my mouth to spill the information, my throat constricts and the words die unspoken. I swallow and try again. No dice.

"What you are waiting for? I give you picture, you give me name."

My hand flies to my throat. I can breathe fine. I just can't say his name.

"Give me name. *Now*."

I take an involuntary step back. Meat matches it with a giant step forward. I move my jaw, trying to make my voice work, but it's no use. My pathetic conscience has hijacked my vocal cords. And judging by Meat's darkening expression, his hands curling into twin sledgehammers, I'd better figure out a con to get that picture and get out before I get pounded. Sadly, I've been so off my game that it didn't occur to me to gather dirt on Meat or his boss, which is going to make conning either or both of them difficult.

Time to stall.

"It's me." I mentally curse my abominable conscience. "I pretended to steal from you so I'd have information to bribe you with. The money's in an offshore account. If you want the number—"

Meat pauses, listening, then grumbles to himself in Albanian and looks at me again—a you-are-about-to-be-dead look that liquifies all my leg muscles. It's probably the last thing all his victims see.

"Moretti. My name's Moretti. I'm the daughter of Alessandra Moretti—granddaughter of Lucrezia Moretti." I'm babbling now, backing up steadily as Meat advances. "If you hurt me, you're a dead man."

Meat fumbles a step but quickly recovers. He either doesn't believe me or he doesn't care. Or, more likely, his boss doesn't. *Crap.*

I force myself to stop retreating and strike a haughty pose, hand on hip, tossing my hair in a perfect imitation of Murphy's girlfriend Bryn.

"You don't really think I came here alone, do you?" I say, projecting my voice like a diva onstage. "I'm willing to call off my guns if you back off." And, icing on the cake, I surreptitiously shine the laser pointer I'd hidden in my pocket for just this purpose on his button-down shirt, just over his heart.

Then I hear a click and feel the cold barrel of a gun pressed behind my right ear. I freeze. It's only been a little over four months since I was shot. A shudder tears through me, and I nearly lose my lunch. Because there's no cavalry coming this time. And even if I give up the real thief, I doubt I'd make it out of this junkyard at this point anyway.

My mind empties. *It is simply time for Plan B.*

Except confessing to the theft *was* my plan B. And revealing my kinship to the Morettis was plan C, and the laser pointer was plan D. I'm on plan freaking E and I got nothing.

"We meet again, grifter."

I swallow a gasp. I don't have to see the speaker to recognize her. I'd know that too-gorgeous sneer anywhere.

Not her. Anybody *but her.*

I pause a beat to gather myself. I can't show weakness. Not if I want to live.

"Han," I say through my teeth, relieved at managing a steady tone, despite the gun. "Nice of you to join us."

Han, enforcer in her own right, and more importantly, Dani's ex-girlfriend, digs the gun in deeper, forcing me to tilt my head to the side. "You know, I detest sarcasm. It's so self-indulgent."

I smirk, ignoring the reality of imminent death in favor of a flawless comeback:

"Dani has no problem with it."

Han pulls away from me and circles into view, gesticulating wildly with her gun. "It's like you're *daring* me to blow your fool head off!"

Okay, so bringing Dani into it was definitely not my best move. But the petty part of me—which, let's be honest, is a rather large part—can't resist needling her ex-girlfriend. And anyway, I'm not the only fool within a two-foot radius.

"Albanians, Han? Really? They're not famous for

following through on their promises to contractors. In fact, they're not famous for allowing contractors to live after the job. Did you think about that?"

Han shifts her stance, pointing her gun at my face. Then she swings a one-eighty and shoots Meat in the side. He roars in pain, dropping the sawed-off shotgun he'd pulled from under his enormous jacket while I was otherwise occupied.

"Run!" Han shouts at me as shots ring out around us.

"Run where?" I shout back, but rather than answer, she darts through piles of trash to an even less well lit area of the junkyard. I leap after her, though probably my better bet is to go the opposite direction. Han loathes me, and I have no idea what price she'll ask for saving my hide. Still, I follow. Mostly because I don't want to face the Albanians alone if I get caught.

I almost lose her when she takes a couple of quick turns in a row, but she slows enough to let me catch up, barely, before taking off again. She's leading me somewhere, and I'm crossing all my fingers that it's not just to a cozier killing ground.

Our pursuers are gaining on us, though, and I can hear her cursing my slowness. Not that I'm actually slow. My feet are flying over the uneven ground. But not fast enough, if the grunts and shouting around every corner is anything to go by.

"Haul your ass, grifter, or I'm leaving it behind!"

I hurl myself around a pile of rusted fenders and

finally see our intended destination: a Suzuki GW250 parked in a grassy clearing on the outer edge of the junk-yard. I skid to a stop while Han grabs the handlebars and swings a leg over the side.

"Get on!"

"I'm not going anywhere with you," I say, just as a bullet punches through the fender behind me.

I holster my pride and clamber up behind Han on the motorbike. She rips open the throttle, and we tear a circular patch in the grass as we swerve through the ditch and up onto the road. Shots zing past us as a deluge of mobsters boils out from behind the junk piles. I wrap my arms tighter around Han's ribs as she zooms to a break-neck speed. I'm conscious of my unhelmeted head, fear of death by asphalt warring with fear of the firearms still going off behind me. But as the sound of Albanian curses fades with increasing distance, I grudgingly acknowledge the need for expediency.

Han rescued me. Han rescued *me*. How did she know I was there? Why would she even bother? She thinks I stole Dani from her, and I suppose it's possible I did. She should have been rock-paper-scissors-ing the Albanians for the first shot, not pulling me out. I'll have to wait to get the story out of her, though. The wind whipping by would toss my words to the ozone.

Soon the scenery starts looking familiar. Chicago's ritzy Wicker Park is my territory. St. Agatha's, the private school I attend, is right around the corner, as well as my office.

I sit up, pulling away from her blood-red jacket as she slows the bike to a more city-friendly speed. When she pulls into the parking lot of Cafe Ballou, I hop off and grab the handlebar to keep her from disappearing.

"What the hell, Han? How did you know my office is above the Ballou? How did you know where I was, and why did you save me?"

Han frowns at me. "You're welcome, grifter. Glad I could be of service. You can be sure I'll think twice before doing it again."

I twist the handle sharply toward me, forcing her off balance. "Do you know where Dani is?"

"No!" she yells at me. "Now let go of my damn bike."

"Not until you tell me what's going on." I'm determined to get answers tonight, even if they're not the answers I actually want.

Han hisses at me as she straightens the handlebar against my resistance. "Dani asked me to watch your back. She paid her debt to me, and now I owe her."

I lean forward, my face bare millimeters from Han's. "I'll ask you one more time. Do. You. Know. Where. She. Is."

Han's glare is unwavering as she huffs in outrage. "No. She was here. A few weeks ago. She—"

"She was here? In Chicago?"

"Keep up, grifter. She paid her debt, and things went sideways. She pulled me out, so—"

"She was here and she didn't—?" I stop, biting my lip against the sudden wobble in my voice.

Get a grip, Julep.

Han smirks at me, giving up our tug of war for the bike to sit up and cross her arms. "Maybe she's already moved on."

I flinch. Okay, I probably deserved that. "That still doesn't explain why you're shooting up Albanians to keep me in the realm of the living."

Han's smirk slips into a pensive expression. "She asked me to protect you."

For the second time tonight, my legs turn jello-y. "What did she say exactly?"

Han sighs. "She said, 'Keep her safe for me.'" She waves off my next question, clearly anticipating it. "I got the impression it was an indefinite arrangement."

I suck in a breath and hold it, blinking. My exhale is an explosion of questions.

"How was she? Did she seem okay? Was she—?"

"She's alive," she interrupts, her voice thick with her own emotion.

I swallow hard and let go of the bike. But instead of leaving, she pulls her phone out of her jacket pocket. Her fingers glide over the screen as she says, "I'm texting you my number. Don't use it unless you literally have no other choice."

"How did you get my number?"

Han stares at me flatly. "I've already said it three times now. Dani asked me to watch your back, so I've been keeping tabs on you since she left a few weeks ago. That means surveillance. Phone number's the first thing I crack. Give me some damn credit for being competent at my job."

"What do you mean she paid her debt—"

"I've had enough of junior twenty questions," she says, then mutters to herself as puts her bike in gear. "Can't believe I agreed to this."

Then she backs up and peels out of the Ballou parking lot.

THE CATFISH

Once she's out of sight, I climb the galvanized steel staircase hugging the Ballou's exterior wall. Normally, I'd go through the Ballou proper to get to my office, grabbing a cup of joe on the way. But it's late, and the Ballou closed hours ago.

I unlock the outer door and enter the upper hallway. My office is the first door on the left from the back entrance, and it's been long enough now that I barely notice the *J.D. & Associates, Private Investigation and Security Testing* printed on the inset frosted window.

I shoulder open the door—it has a tendency to stick—and drop my coat on the couch. It's hard to ignore the random detritus scattered around the room. Small piles of computer bits and stacks of manila folders and random equipment for making forgeries mingle with the occasional empty coffee cup and random trigonometry textbook.

J.D. & Associates mostly ferrets out insurance scams, but occasionally we test security systems, both online and off, for companies wanting to pit an experienced team of crackers against the latest and best security measures the tech industry has to offer. There have been a couple we couldn't crack, but not many. Sam's a sore loser.

Tonight, though, I need to use our considerable resources to get Hajdari, the Albanian drug addict, and his family to safety. Luckily for me, all it takes is a phone call.

I sit behind my chipped, thrift-store special oak desk, and dial the number.

"Hey, Mike?" I say when he picks up. "I may have developed a slight Albanian problem..."

Twenty minutes of Lecture de Mike Ramirez™ later, I end the call and lean back in my chair with a groan. I didn't even tell him about the junkyard debacle. If I had, I'd be on a one-way trip to Witness Protection. Instead, I carefully crafted a story to make sure Hajdari got offered that trip instead. Here's hoping he's smart enough to take it. Anyway, Mike's on his way to pick me up, which means I'll get a fifteen-minute continuation lecture on the way home. Joy.

I stare at the ceiling, thinking of my dad and what he'd do in my situation. Not the Albanian situation–the missing Dani situation. But it isn't much of a leap to get to the answer. Mom was in trouble once when I was thirteen.

He left me alone for two weeks without a word while he tracked her down and helped her disappear. He'd do whatever it took to fix it, even give her up.

You, me, and sixty-three.

Ha. What a joke.

The office phone on my desk rings suddenly, scaring the bejeezus out of me. I lean forward and nearly fumble the handset. Hardly anyone calls the office landline. Which means this is either a new client or a robocall. I'm betting the latter, given the hour. But sadly, I have to answer either way, just in case it's the former.

"J.D. & Associates, Julep speaking. How may I direct your call?"

Sometimes I like to throw people off by actually sounding professional.

"Yeah, hi. My name's Anton Walker. Are you the kid PI?"

"I'm hanging up now."

"Wait! Wait. That came out… What I meant was, are you the private investigator who helps kids?"

"What."

"The PI who helps kids."

"Lots of PIs help kids."

"Yeah, but…it's not the same. Word is you help kids when adults won't. When they can't."

I breathe in deeply through my nose. It's like he thinks I'm some quirky folk hero.

"I just do my job," I say, finally.

"I can pay," he hurries to assure me. "I mean, I can pay some. How much do you charge?"

This is what I get for answering the phone.

"Let's back up a bit, shall we? What seems to be the problem?"

"My dad's getting catfished. I'm sure of it, but I just can't prove it."

"What makes you think he's being catfished? Is the person avoiding face-to-face meetings or video calls?"

"She says she's in Witness Protection, and that she travels a lot to stay off the grid, specifically in places that don't have good reception. But she texts and calls, and she sent a selfie once."

"Did you try a reverse Google-image search of the photo?"

"Yeah, I did the basics—suggestions I found online."

"And?"

"And everything checks out," he admitted grudgingly. "Not that there's much to go on."

"Has she asked your dad for money?"

"Not that I know of. We don't have any even if she did. He's a single parent with a job at the liquor store for minimum wage. I think she may have given *him* money once or twice."

What kind of catfish gives money to their victim? Or even goes to all this trouble for a single mark? Most cons are false fronts—rickety set dressing at best that would blow over from a stiff cough from the audience. Grifters don't have time for anything elaborate, and anyway, it'd be a waste. If a mark sees through the illusion, we just hot foot it out the door and on to the next mark, who is hopefully a few degrees less savvy. My point being, I don't see what he's seeing here.

But instead of all that, I say, "How old are you?" Not because I need to know, but because I'm curious.

"Fifteen," he says. "Sixteen next March."

"And what's your dad like?"

"He's nice. A little too nice," Anton says. "He can't say no when people ask him for things."

"I'm assuming you've already tried taking this matter to the relevant authorities?"

"I've tried the cops, I've tried hotlines. I even tried Dr. Phil. But no one believes us."

"Us?"

"There's five of us kids. I'm the oldest, but no one takes us seriously."

"And you all believe this is happening?"

"Yes," he says simply. "I know it doesn't sound like she's a catfish. But she is. I'm sure of it."

"Well, I'm going to need a bit more than your gut feeling to go on if I take your case," I say, searching my desk and then Murphy's for a writing implement. "Can you come into the office tomorrow? Say, six-ish?"

"I don't live in Chicago," Anton says.

"You don't?" I say, surprised enough to abandon my pencil search. "Where do you live?"

I expect him to say Naperville or Schaumburg. Or maybe even Milwaukee. I do not expect him to say,

"Detroit."

"Detroit, as in *Michigan?*" I say, aghast.

"Yeah."

"How the hell did you hear about me all the way out in Michigan?"

"I read about you on Reddit."

"Reddit?" I squeak.

"Someone from Cali posted that—"

"Someone from *California* posted about me?"

That's it. I might as well close shop completely. I'm never going to be able to fly under the radar again. I take a deep breath or three to calm down.

"Okay. Let's just put a pin in that for now. How about you tell me why you called *me* specifically? I'm sure there are any number of competent PIs that could help you from the comfort and convenience of your own state."

"You mean aside from you being the person kids go to when they have a problem?"

"Humor me."

"Well, the catfish lives in Chicago. Or at least says she does."

"She does?" I say, finally perking up. Maybe this train wreck of a phone call wasn't for nothing. "Is she here now, or traveling?"

"Traveling, but should be back any day."

"One last question, and then I'll think about it," I say,

fiddling with some obscure chunk of circuitry Murphy had left on his desk. "What's it to you?"

"What do you mean?"

"If she's not hurting him, and may even be helping him, then what's it to you if he has a relationship with a woman who doesn't exist?"

There's a silence that stretches oddly on the other end of the line. So much so that I almost repeat the question. But then he answers, and my blood runs cold.

"She's pretending to be our mom, who died eight years ago."

THE NEXT MORNING, Mike clomps down the stairs like an eight-hundred-pound gorilla, lumbering into the kitchen to kiss Angela's cheek and grab his commuter mug of coffee before scooping up his jacket and his briefcase and shouting at me over his shoulder.

"Let's go, kid! Traffic's already abysmal."

I breathe a sigh of relief as I drag my butt off the barstool and slither into my coat. At least he didn't say "train's leaving the station" like he usually does.

"C'mon, Julep! Get the lead out!"

I groan and shoulder my book bag, snagging another commuter mug that Angela's just refilled for me off the bar. I don't kiss her, but I would if I could feel my face. I definitely wasn't made for mornings.

Lily's already in the backseat, scrolling through TikTok on her phone, looking fresh as a daisy. I envy her youth and vitality for about point-two seconds. Then I remember that I would rather die than go through eighth grade again.

"Sunglasses are a bit dramatic, don't you think?" Lily asks without looking up from her phone. "It's raining."

"Gen Z just thinks they know everything, don't they?" I say to Mike, who's paying no attention to us whatsoever.

"What?" he says, distracted by a left turn through oncoming traffic.

"All right, Grandma," Lily interjects, rolling her eyes. "Pretty sure you're also technically Gen Z."

"I am every generation."

Lily snorts, and goes back to her phone.

I take a long drag from my second coffee of the day and pull out my own phone. It's too damn early for work, but I'd be lying if I said I could get the case of the mom-fish out of my head.

Why go to the trouble of impersonating a dead woman? And, yeah, she's probably dead. Her death record was the first thing I looked up after I got off the phone with Anton. I suppose it's possible she faked her own death, but that's not easy to do. And even if Anton's mom did fake her death, then why come back, acting like nothing happened? What possible explanation could she give that would make any sense?

"Got a job for you, Lils," I say around a massive yawn.

"'Bout time," she says, her lips turning up in a quirk of a smile. She's been coming out of her shell more and more the last few weeks. Her brother's death and her parents' subsequent incarcerations may have upended her life completely, but since our shared escape from the hitman her mom hired to assassinate me, she seems to blame me less. She's even hugged me once or twice without trying to stab me in the back—which is, frankly, a first for her family. "You've been letting the boys take over too much lately."

"I've been busy." As she very well knows.

"So? What's the job?"

"Job? What job?" Mike asks from the driver's seat.

"Nothing to do with the Albanians, I swear. Totally unrelated."

"What Albanians?" Lily asks.

"I'll tell you later," I say. "In any case, it's not about them. I've got a catfish client."

"Your client's a catfish?" Mike asks, shooting me a confused look through the mirror.

"No, the client's dad is being catfished," I explain. Then I give them a rundown of everything I know so far.

"Detroit?" Lily says when I get to that part. "You have clients calling from other states now?"

"Believe me, I am not thrilled."

"What do you need me to do?" she says, clearly enjoying my discomfort at my sudden notoriety far too much.

I ignore the insubordination for now. "I don't buy for a minute that Anton's mom faked her death to enter WITSEC."

"What's WITSEC again?"

"Witness protection program," Mike offers from the front. "You know, that thing that Julep should really be in?"

"WITSEC is just a handy excuse for avoiding video calls," I say, ignoring the peanut gallery. "And it's not like we can just check to see if she's in it. They don't keep centralized records about program participants. Even if they did, I wouldn't want any of us hacking or grifting our way into it. Some things we're far better off never knowing."

"So dead end?"

"Not exactly. Even if we can't see the fire, we can still smell the smoke."

"Meaning...?"

"Whoever it is wants something, and they want it bad enough to go to a lot of effort mimicking this woman."

"Maybe the catfish isn't just targeting Anton's family," Lily supplies, her eyes lighting up as she catches on. "Maybe they're targeting other people in Anton's mom's life. But why?"

"That's what I need you to find out," I say, texting her Anton's number. "Get what you can about Anton's real mom's death, starting by interviewing him about it. Also see if you can dig up any information on friends of hers.

You're looking for anyone who might have a motive to pull a con of this size. Bonus points if they're connected to Chicago in some way."

"On it," she says, stowing her phone in an exterior pocket of her book bag as we pull up outside of St. Agatha's. Then she turns her sweet, guileless smile on our driver. "Mike?"

He sighs heavily. "I have *one* connection in the Detroit PD, but they're not homicide, so I'm not promising anything."

"Thanks, Mike," she says, releasing her seatbelt and leaning forward to hug him from behind his seat. "You're my hero."

"Hey, I thought I was your hero," I say. I mean, I did take a bullet for her.

"I can have more than one hero," she says. Then she opens the door and climbs out.

I slide across the bench seat and get out after her.

"I'll be late tonight, so take the train home," Mike calls out after us.

I salute him through the open door, then close it behind me. I fall into step next to Lily as we climb the stairs to the large, wooden front door to the school. I pull it open for her, and she slips into the noisy hallway interior ahead of me. I fist bump her, and we head in opposite directions.

I take a detour from first period, towards the Brockman room and the administrative wing. The Albanians were less than helpful, but they're not the only crime syndicate in town. I think it's telling that I would rather face the Albanians than my own alleged grandmother, but then I don't owe the Albanians any favors. I do owe the Morettis a favor, and it's making my entire body itch from the inside out.

"Are you coming or going, Ms. Dupree?" Janet, Sister Rasmussen's administrative assistant, calls out to me—not for the first time. This office is often the last place I go before crap hits the fan, so I hesitate at the threshold every time I end up here. I take a deep breath and walk into the sitting area.

"Can I get you anything?" she asks blandly, gesturing to the small sofa where guests wait to be announced. "Water, tea, Xanax?"

I smile at Janet. She's usually uptight and jittery, like a church mouse in a demon's lair. I'm glad she's getting used to me enough that she's letting her guard down. Makes me feel like I'm winning her over to the dark side—or the medium-gray side, as it were.

"She's been expecting you," Janet continues with a smirk, handing me a cup of room-temperature water I didn't ask for.

"Weird, since I didn't decide to come until a minute ago."

"Ms. Dupree," Sister Rasmussen's voice carries through the door to the right of the sitting room.

I guzzle the water in three swallows and hand the empty cup back to Janet, and she pats my shoulder.

"Godspeed," she says.

I straighten my shoulders, and head toward my doom.

It's not that Sister Rasmussen has ever been anything but unfailingly kind to me. She's helped me out of a few jams, even. But if she really is my grandmother, then she's the head of the oldest, bloodiest crime family in history, with tentacles wrapped around the finances of every country with more than two coins to rub together. She's the devil in nun's clothing. Only a fool would make a deal with her, and I've already made at least two.

"Good morning," Sister Rasmussen says politely, offering me what I've come to see as my chair with one hand, while raising a china teacup with the other. "I trust you slept well."

"I haven't slept a full night since I got shot," I say, though it has nothing to do with getting shot and everything to do with Dani leaving with Petrov.

"I'm sorry to hear that," she says mildly. "Have you—"

"Yes," I say. "I've seen all the doctors, thanks. But there's only one thing that'll cure it, and I'm hoping you can help me get it."

"Bold of you to ask for assistance when you have yet to fulfill your obligation for the last favor we granted you."

"You said you'd give me time to recover before I had to start the internship with Brillion," I say, referring to my part of the bargain for Ralph's help in escaping a contract killer last summer.

"Yes, and I stand by that. Are you well enough to return to the game?"

"Depends on the game," I say truthfully. "Are there guns involved?"

"No," she says, though there's a slight enough hesitation that my grifter senses twinge.

"You know, if I had a little extra incentive, I'd be more motivated to jump in."

"What incentive did you have in mind?"

Time for the hard part. Not the asking, but the outing of Dani's connection to me. The more the Morettis know about my weaknesses, the more easily they'll be able to control me in the future. But there's nothing for it. I have to get her back, and I have tried literally everything else. I have no choice.

"Nikolai Petrov has something I want."

"Yes, I am aware of your problem," she says, grimacing slightly. "I do keep tabs on you, my dear."

I shudder involuntarily. I'm not surprised by that, given that Ralph's been spying on me through his supposed friendship with my dad at Sister Rasmussen's behest for literal years. Doesn't make me hate it any less.

"Believe me, I wouldn't be asking if I had anywhere else to turn," I say, truthfully, because she's the kind of person who responds to honesty with honesty. The last thing I want is for her to lie to me more than she already has. Grifter rule #104: If you can't keep your enemies in your rearview, then keep them in your passenger's seat.

"I'll see what I can do," she says, folding her hands in her lap. "In the meantime, it's time for you to rejoin the land of the living."

"I'm ready," I say with more bravado than believability.

"Are you?" she raises an eyebrow.

"If it gets me closer to finding her...then, yeah."

11

THE WHITEBOARD

"You sure about this?" Sam asks, as he drives me in his Volvo to the address Janet gave me for the Brillion office.

"If she really is my grandmother, she probably doesn't want to hurt me," I say, looking out the window at the waning light. It's only the last period of the school day, but the shadows are growing in strength.

"I'm hearing a lot of 'ifs' and 'probablys,'" he says. "Did Mike sign off on this?"

Sam Seward, best friend and best hacker I've ever met, is increasingly becoming more my nursemaid than my business partner. He worries. A lot. Probably justifiably. I realize I'm a mess. And since Sam's been my best friend and confidante since grade school, he obviously realizes it, too.

"Mike is blissfully unaware of Sister Rasmussen's

extracurricular activities, and I'd like to keep it that way," I say with a significant look at my driver. "If he had any idea that Sister Rasmussen is maybe, potentially, more-than-likely my grandmother, and more importantly, the crime boss of the century, I wouldn't be allowed within ten miles of St. Agatha's."

"Keeping secrets from Mike hasn't historically gone well for you," Sam notes. Helpfully.

"This doesn't count as keeping secrets, because we don't actually have proof that Sister Rasmussen is Lucrezia Moretti, nor has she admitted it. As far as any of us know *for sure*, she's just the president of St. Agatha's Preparatory School."

Sam snorts. "Is it weird that I find your convoluted anti-logic comforting?"

"Not at all," I say, smirking in spite of myself. "Means I'm in control of the narrative, and who doesn't find that comforting?"

Sam outright laughs at that. And that's what I really find comforting. An easy, drama-free drive with my best friend. Saying that we've had our issues is an understatement of epic proportions, but his return from military school a few months ago has given us a chance to adjust to the new versions of each other. He's still my right hand, and I'd still kill tigers for him. But we're no longer so tangled up in each other that we've excluded literally everyone else. We've evolved into actual individuals.

Exceptionally messed up and morally questionable individuals, but hey, it's a place to start.

The Volvo rolls to a stop next to an unassuming strip mall.

"You sure this is the place?" he says.

I unlock my phone and double-check the address Janet gave me as I left Sister Rasmussen's office.

"Unless Janet is pranking me, this is it," I say and open the door.

"Want me to come in with you and check it out?" Sam asks, scanning our surroundings in his mirrors.

"Nah," I say as I loop my book bag onto my shoulders. "Keep an eye on your phone though. I'll text if I need an extraction."

"Deal," he says, and I get out.

The front for Brillion Industries is a glass door with a *No Solicitors* sticker and translucent sun-shade that's seen better days. The flimsy deadbolt couldn't keep out a Girl Scout-cookie peddler, let alone a hoard of law enforcement officers. Hardly the fortress I'd expect for what I assume to be the headquarters of a criminal consortium.

"Can I help you?" says a scruffy schlub in a Hawaiian shirt behind the 1960s-era circulation desk. I'd bet my last coffee that the orange-beige-speckled carpet is original as well.

"I'm here for the Brillion internship," I say. "Sister Rasmussen sent me."

It's not exactly a secret code word, but it should get me where I need to go.

The man picks up his desk-phone handset and presses a button on the phone's base. When whoever's on the other end picks up, he says, "Yep," and hangs up.

"Have a seat," he says, retrieving a copy of *PC Gamer* from on top of the blotter next to the phone.

I comply without asking how long the wait will be. They can take all the time in the world, for all I care.

I pull out my phone and text Lily.

> Any news on Mama Catfish?

A minute or two later, she responds,

> Interview with client scheduled 4pm. Not much online. Murphy digging into dark web.

It's been less than a day, so none of us have had much of a chance to investigate. But I'm already regretting taking this case. The PI who helps kids? Who the hell is spreading this crap, and how can I get them to stop? No one in California should know my name. No one in *Chicago* should know my name, outside of St. Agatha's. My dad is going to have a coronary when he hears about this.

"Grifter," says a familiar voice.

I look up from my phone to see Victoria Febbi, arms folded, glaring down at me. Good old Victoria, lately of

Bar63 bartender fame. But more to the point, admitted Moretti conspirator, who more hindered than helped me on the disastrous NWI case.

"Vicky," I say. "Nice to see you again."

"Wish I could say the same," she says with a snort.

"Happy to leave if you'd rather not have me," I say, gesturing with my thumb to the much preferable out of doors.

"Orders are orders." She gestures for me to precede her past the desk and cheesy inspirational office posters to the one-door elevator with a single button pointing down.

"I think I've seen this movie," I say, as I push the down button. "A secret, state-of-the-art, underground bunker? Are there aliens? Do I get a black suit and one of those blinky, memory-eraser things?"

"Is it physically possible for you to take anything seriously? Even for five minutes?" she asks.

"Where's the fun in that?"

Then conversation halts as we wait for the elevator to reach its destination. It's either an incredibly slow elevator, or we're going to pop out the other side into China. I glance at my phone. Zero bars. Lovely. So much for texting for help.

"Any chance I can get the wifi password?" I ask her.

She holds out her hand. I sigh heavily and relinquish my phone.

"You'll get it back at the end of your shift," she says,

stowing my lifeline in her jeans pocket. "We do a lot of sensitive work here."

"I'll bet."

"You'll sign a non-disclosure agreement before the tour."

"You'd actually trust a grifter with just a non-disclosure agreement?"

"It's a unique non-disclosure agreement," Victoria says with a sharp smile.

Probably contractually guarantees I'll have to give up body parts if I spill their secrets.

"If it's a problem, I can just let a classmate have my spot."

"Our next pick would be your friend Sam Seward. You really want him in here instead of you?"

The threat is subtle, I'll give her that. And effective, since it shuts me right up. I'm not sending anyone into the Morettis' clutches, least of all my best friend.

The elevator stops—finally—and it's such a relief that I actually let Victoria have the last word. When the doors slide open, I blink in temporary confusion. As much as I'd joked about an underground bunker, I hadn't actually expected to see quite so much concrete and fluorescence.

It looks as big as the entire strip mall, parking lot included. It's two levels at least, with who knows how many offshoot wings extending down surrounding corridors. People in office attire flit between desks while others hunch behind computer monitors, staring at screens and tapping on keyboards.

"Come on," Victoria says. "Conference room's this way."

I follow her from the elevator bay down a set of metal stairs to the main floor. People look up at us with curiosity and more than a little distrust. I stick out like a sore thumb in my Catholic school-girl uniform. I might as well be wearing pigtails and skipping down the aisle with a lollipop in my mouth. If I'm lucky, it'll make them underestimate me, even if they've already been briefed about who I am.

She leads me to a small conference room just off the main floor. Half the wall is windows, looking out onto the rows of desks in precise formation. I suspect this is intentional. The worst thing they could do is stick me in a room and lose line of sight. I'm pretty good at sleight-of-hand when I want to be.

She opens the door for me, and I enter, looking around at the stacks of banker boxes overflowing with manila folders and reams of printer paper.

"Don't tell me. You're giving me shredding duty. You know there are laws against destroying evidence of foul play."

"If only it were that simple," she says. "Get comfortable. You're going to be here a while."

"Doing what?"

"Your first internship project."

I pick up a nearby folder and flip it open. "Alanzo Moretti?"

"Your third cousin, twice-removed," she says. Then she gestures to the rest of the boxes. "All of this is intel on the Moretti family. You're behind, thanks to your NWI distraction over the summer. Consider this your chance to read up on the family."

"Wow. Police reports instead of photo albums? Touching. And don't you mean *our* family, cousin?"

She shrugs. "Somehow we thought this would pique your interest more than reminiscences around a campfire."

"You underestimate my love of campfires."

"I'm sure you'll get over it."

"Where's the NDA?"

"You signed it by walking out of that elevator."

"What are the terms?"

"Do what we tell you and keep your mouth shut. Or else."

"Fair," I say, glad it's not worse. "When's the tour?"

"That was the tour. Bathroom's around the corner. If you feel the need to ask for anything, don't."

"Got it."

She shuts the door with a click behind her, leaving me to wonder exactly how long my "shift" is. But I'd be lying if I said I wasn't interested in the work. I turn to survey the literal mountains of boxes hugging the walls of the small conference room. It's warm in here with the door closed, the HVAC system doing its best with the recycled air this far underground. I shed my v-neck sweater and unbutton my collar, rolling my sleeves up to my elbows. I'll definitely pack a change of clothes and an extra bottle of water for tomorrow.

Then I take a seat and start reading.

TWO HOURS and a pulsating headache later, I'm standing in the strip mall parking lot as the Volvo rolls up to rescue me.

"Well?" Sam says, when I get in.

"I'm alive," I say wearily, leaning back against the headrest and closing my eyes.

"That good?"

"Actually, surprisingly, yeah," I say, rubbing my temple. He pulls out of the parking lot and heads toward home.

"Care to share?"

"I technically signed an NDA."

"*You* signed an NDA?"

"It's more an understanding than an actual contract. But it's neither here nor there, as I have no intention of abiding by it."

"There's the Julep we know and love," he says with a smile. "I was worried for a minute there."

"They stuck me in a room full of files about the Morettis."

"That's...weird," he says, perking up. "Why?"

"Catch me up on the family business, I guess," I say.

"Did you get a read on the facility or the employees? What do they do there?"

"Maybe you missed the part where they stuck me in a room full of files about the Morettis. I saw a cubicle farm of computers and a handful of office peons before they shuffled me into the conference room and shut the door. But I'll tell you this, it's big, and it's gotta be fifty yards underground. Which means, I'm cut off from communications when I'm down there."

He frowns. "I don't like that."

"Me neither. But if they wanted to hurt me, they'd have done it already. Instead, they've saved my life. Multiple times. So it's probably about as safe down there as it is at St. Agatha's."

"For now," he says.

"For now," I agree.

We pull up to the Ballou and get out. I buy him a mocha—or rather, I have Yaji put it on my tab—and then we mosey up the stairs to the office, catching up on the rest of the day.

"Any progress on the catfish case?" I ask as we walk in the door.

Murphy and Lily are already present, Murphy at his

desk under the window, Lily sprawled across the teal couch, her feet bouncing to the rhythm of whatever she's listening to on her earbuds. I tap her on the head as I pass, and she swivels on her butt to sit upright, taking out her tunes.

"I'm so glad you asked," Murphy says, springing out of his chair and heading toward the closet. Whenever Murphy's this excited, I can pretty much guarantee I'm not going to like whatever it is he's excited about.

He reaches the folding doors of the closet and tugs them apart, revealing a three-foot by four-foot dry-erase board on wheels. He maneuvers it free of the closet doors and pulls it to the center of the room. Then he stands to the side and throws his hands up in a showman's *ta-da!* gesture.

"What is that?" I say, each word carrying the weight of my unadulterated disgust.

"It's a whiteboard."

"I can see it's a whiteboard," I say, shooting an angry glare at my AV specialist. "You know how I feel about sleuthing, Murphy."

"I have news for you, boss—private investigating *is* sleuthing."

"Private investigating does not require the *appearance* of sleuthing."

Murphy matches my glare with a steely one of his own, as Lily swoops in and snags the blue dry-erase marker from his grip.

"Grow up, Julep," Lily says, uncapping the marker and

writing some kind of heading on the board. *Suspects*, it says. And it's then that I notice the rest of the content either taped or written on the surface. "It was either this or a bulletin board, and we figured you'd burst a blood vessel if we started looping red string around pushpins."

"Looks like you've been busy," Sam jumps in, clearly attempting to get us back on track.

"Anton wasn't exactly a font of useful information," Lily says. "The Witness Protection excuse has given our catfish a lot of rope in terms of dodging visuals. She has talked to the kids, and from what they remember, it sounds like her. But the eight-year time gap between her death and this rando popping up out of nowhere makes memory questionable."

"Not to mention," Murphy adds. "With the AI that's out on the market now, it'd be easy for a catfish to mimic her, even with just a handful of recorded clips to clone from."

"They'd have to get a recording of her, though," I point out. "Could be a way to track them."

Murphy looks thoughtful. "Maybe, but with the volume of video that gets posted to socials, I wouldn't be surprised if we never find a connection."

"What about reverse phone lookup?" Sam asks.

"Dead end," Lily replies. "The catfish used a VOIP service and blocked their outgoing caller ID. They said it was a safety measure to keep off bad-guy radar."

"Did they happen to say who the bad guys were?"

"The catfish won't talk about any of that, claiming they don't want to endanger the family by accidentally giving away too much information. All they'll say is that something happened, and they had to play dead and join WITSEC because of it."

I sigh and flop into my chair. It's not as if I don't have ninety-nine other problems.

"Okay, enough with what you haven't got. Tell me what you have got."

Lily's smile has a distinct flavor of self-satisfaction. I think I may be rubbing off on her a bit too much. She moves to the other side of the whiteboard and points to a picture of a pretty, black-haired woman a little younger than Angela and Mike. She's looking off camera into the distance while the sun sets in the background.

"Before Carmen Walker was Carmen Walker, she was Carmen Elena Mariana Santiago."

"Which matters because?"

"Because her father was Tomas Fernando Luis Santiago, one of the regional officers for the Juarez cartel in Mexico."

"Is that why she died?"

"According to Anton, the cops don't think so," Lily says, pointing to another picture beneath Carmen's, a screengrab from a video showing the taillights of a white Plymouth speeding off into the night. "Looks like a hit and run from surveillance footage. It could be that the person knew her, but the investigation didn't find any evidence to support that."

"Well, it ain't easy leaving a *familia criminal*, I can tell you." I absently trace the wood grain on my desk with a nail, thinking. "Did Anton know anything about that side of the family?"

Lily shakes her head again. "He says she cut ties with the cartel well before he was even born, and he never noticed any sign of them trying to contact her. He thinks his grandfather, Tomas, is dead now, and he has no idea what other relatives he might have still in the cartel. But otherwise she was a kindergarten teacher who lived in the suburbs with her family. No connection that we can find to anything that might necessitate her faking her own death."

"Well, it's something. Have Anton see what he can dig up in his dad's things, or even better his mom's things. Sam and I have a little fishing of our own to do."

"Fishing?" Sam asks.

"And shopping," I say.

"Fishing and shopping?"

"And maybe dinner," I add, taking advantage while I can. "You're buying, of course."

"Of course," he says, sardonically. The eyeroll is implied.

12

THE CARTEL

The library at St. Agatha's is loaded in more ways than one. Books line the shelves in hardcover armor, like regimented soldiers staging their defense against our generation's withering attention spans. Students fill the seats. Most of them are our classmates, juniors cramming for the upcoming college entrance exams. St. Agatha's keeps its library doors open late during exams week, staffed with whatever student-teacher they can wrangle into staying after hours.

But the library is also stuffed to the gills with illegal drugs, and I don't just mean the head librarian's private stash of Ambien that her doctor didn't officially approve.

"Hey, Jimmy," I say to James Sullivan, the student-teacher for the history and psychology department, as Sam and I saunter up to the circulation desk. "How's things?"

Jimmy's eyes widen when he sees me, and he frantically points at the QUIET PLEASE poster on the wall next to the desk.

I take the hint and make a show of tearing off a sheet of paper from the call slip pad and turning it over face-down on the desk. Then I grab a pencil stub from the nearby cup and write the following message:

Relax. Not here to whistle. Calling in my favor.

Then I fold the slip in half and hand it to him. He reads quickly, crumples the note, and stuffs it in his pocket. He takes out a small, red business card with tiny black printing on it and hands it to me. On it is a complicated grid that I'm certain has something to do with ordering a type and amount of a variety of illicit substances. Judging from the number of rows and columns, he's got a whole pharmacy back there.

I return the card. No point in being wasteful.

"That's not what I need," I say in nearly a whisper.

He gestures with his head to a side door that leads out into the hall. We'll have to go the long way to meet him to avoid looking suspicious. No one's supposed to go behind the circulation desk if they don't actually work for the library. It's part of why Jimmy chose the student-assistant gig that he did. The library's the safest place on school grounds for his stash. Plus, he's a giant Faulkner-d.

"What do you want?" he asks, just shy of hostile, as he joins us in the hall. It's probably due to nerves. Everyone gets sweaty when I show up to collect.

"I need to talk to someone in the Juarez cartel."

Jimmy blinks at me owlishly through round glasses that look like they're from the Victorian era.

"Have you looked at a map recently? Do you know how far we are from Mexico? I move local product. I'm not part of importing."

"Yeah, but you know a guy who knows a guy, right?"

He makes a few noises of protest, but after a minute, he comes around. "I...*may* know someone who's cousins with a lawyer who does the occasional contract work for La Linea, but—"

"We'll take it," I say, not interested in hearing his slew of limitations and caveats. I hand him my business card. "Have whoever you can get from La Linea call me at this number. Tonight. It's about Tomas Santiago."

"Tonight! I can't just—"

I take a casual step into his personal space.

"Jimmy, Jimmy, Jimmy..." I say, straightening his already straight tie. "I believe in you."

The implied threat that I'll spill all his secrets if he doesn't come through doesn't actually need to be said. He knows it, as all my clients know it. When I ask for my favor, you'd better deliver, or else you go down for the very thing you paid me to do.

I can't say I feel great about strong-arming Jimmy, especially when it involves a cartel. But I need the short-cut, and Jimmy's who I have on the hook. Besides, it's true that I believe in him. Given the right incentive, people can work miracles. And right now, I have miracles of my own to perform.

I lead Sam back down the hall toward the exit, as Jimmy dutifully pulls out his phone.

LATER, between sips of my Orange Julius Tropical Tango smoothie, I say to Sam, "Points for keeping your disapproval to yourself."

In truth, he'd kept his disapproval so much to himself that he hadn't spoken beyond monosyllables for the entire walk from the St. Aggie's library to the Water Tower Place food court we are now enjoying the spoils of.

"Telling you never makes a shred of difference, so I figure why bother?" he says with the barest hint of sullen.

I nudge his shin lightly under the formica-topped table. "Just because I never listen to you doesn't mean I don't need you to call me on my crap. Sometimes it helps me brainstorm next steps."

"You mean, the even more hare-brained thing you could do instead?"

"Yeah, that one."

He sighs, folding his arms across his broad chest. "I'm not happy about getting Jimmy noticed by a legit cartel. I'm not happy doing business with Jimmy in the first place. He's not our typical collaborator. The stuff he deals can actually hurt people."

"I know, I know. You're right. But let's focus on the positives, shall we?"

"Like what?"

"Like getting *ourselves* noticed by a legit cartel?" I say, with a rimshot grin.

Sam groans and sinks in his plastic chair, scrubbing his fingers through curly black hair that has *finally* grown back from the severe military cut he got when he left for Giles Academy last semester.

"Why do I get the feeling you're enjoying this?" he says.

I suck in a breath as my heart lurches to the side.

"I'm not enjoying any part of this, Sam." Trying to focus on anything but finding Dani is like trying to reel in a whale with a cooked noodle.

He gives me a long look that says he knows exactly what I'm thinking. Then he sighs heavily and rubs his face as he straightens in his chair. "All right, what do we do now? Wait for La Linea to contact us?"

"Yep."

"And you think they'll just tell us that they were involved in Anton's mother's death eight years ago?"

"Maybe. I mean, what threat are we to them? But even if they won't outright admit to it, what they don't say can sometimes be as telling as what they do say." I sit back and sip more of my smoothie.

"But what if Anton is wrong? What if the catfish really is his mother, she really is hiding out in WITSEC, and we give away to, at the very least, a questionable organization that she's alive? We'd be putting her in danger, even if they're not the ones who want her dead. The more people who know, the bigger the risk to her safety."

"Thanks, genius, I know how WITSEC works. But it doesn't matter. I'm not planning on asking them about Carmen."

"You're not?" Sam asks, a comically perplexed look on his face. I almost snort in amusement, but I manage to rein myself in.

"Of course not," I say, sneakily stealing a fry from a passing tray without attracting attention. "I am not in the habit of negotiating with terrorists."

"Then what is the point of the conversation?"

I pat his cheek with a touch of playful condescension. "You'll see, my faithful sidekick."

He scowls at me.

"In the meantime, I do have some shopping to do. Or rather, you do."

"Really."

"Yes. I figure it's time to upgrade Murphy's stash of listening gizmos."

"What kind of gizmos?"

"Something a little more subtle than a fishing pole."

One hour later, Sam and I are back at the Ballou with a bag full of gear. Murphy's eyes light up like it's Christmas, and he completely abandons his dark-web search to start pawing through the bag.

"You're welcome," I say.

He flaps his hand at me and starts unboxing.

"Not sure why you didn't take him shopping instead of me," Sam says with a snort at Murphy's Gollum-esque huddling around his preciouses.

"Are you kidding? He spent two grand online for x-ray glasses last month. X-ray. Glasses. I'm not taking him into any kind of gadget shop until at least January. My bank account can only take so much."

"The AU508 mobile phone scanner?" Murphy crows. "Score!"

I tune him out and walk up to the whiteboard, shaking my head. A whiteboard, for crying out loud.

My phone buzzes.

No Caller ID

I answer before the second buzz.

"This is Dupree," I say, as I casually stroll to the window. It takes me a minute to spot the SUV with the guy holding a camera with a too-big lens. First the Albanians and now this. Dani would be so furious with me right now. Never thought I'd miss that, but...I do.

"You have thirty seconds," a stranger's voice murmurs in my ear.

I waste a few beats in silence. I've never been very good at following directions.

Sam comes over to stand at my elbow, following my gaze out to the street and to our new friend. He swears softly under his breath.

I leave the window to sit down behind my desk and prop my feet up.

"I have a gift for you," I say.

"Is that so." It wasn't a question. "And how much will this *gift* cost me?"

Not a trace of anything but a midwestern American accent, which likely means I'm talking to a regional grunt of some kind or other. Which isn't necessarily a bad thing. I'd rather La Linea not take me too seriously.

"Not a cent," I say truthfully, picking up a pen from my desk and fiddling with it. I think better with something in my hands. "Just a small, insignificant piece of information."

"If it's insignificant, why do you want it?"

"Insignificant to you. Potentially of interest to a friend of mine."

"And this friend is...?"

"We're getting off track," I say, redirecting the conversation. "Let's focus on the gift for the moment."

"What gift?"

"You've heard of the Capja Albanian syndicate, I'm assuming?"

Here is where I'm taking a bit of a gamble. But if I play

my cards right, I could make more trouble for the Albanians I tangled with in the junkyard while simultaneously prodding the cartel into giving up the information I need. So at his grunt of assent, I continue.

"The Capja dominate the drug trade in Chicago at the moment, but I have it on good authority that they're in a bit of a pickle just now."

"Whose authority?"

"Mine."

"Yeah, I'm not gonna take the word of a grifter."

I grin and lean forward, sliding my feet off of the desk. I love it when a mark doubts my power of persuasion. It makes it all the more satisfying when they crumple to my will, even while fully aware that I'm a con artist.

"I would be happy to give you some proof of their, shall we say, logistical issues," I offer. "But instead, how about we just skip to the part where I give you a bank ledger detailing their supply lines, distribution channels, and pocket politicians?"

Sam starts forward in alarm, gesturing at me to stop, mouthing, *What are you doing?*

I quickly tap mute, waving him off while I turn to Murphy. "You got that scanner up and running yet?"

He shrugs and goes back to tinkering with knobs and antennae. He'd better have it functional before the next phase of my plan, or this conversation will be for naught.

I tap unmute and tune back into the conversation.

"...curious to know how you came by that ledger."

"An unexpected windfall from an unrelated assignment."

"You seem to have quite a few irons in the fire at the moment."

"A typical Tuesday, if I'm honest."

"And you just stumbled upon this ledger during this unrelated assignment?"

"I did. And now the Capja syndicate is—perhaps understandably, given the outcome of that assignment—a little put out with me."

"Ah. I see."

"So it wouldn't be a terrible thing if they were to encounter a bit of a distraction."

"A distraction like La Linea encroaching on their territory?"

"Encroaching is such a negative word. I was thinking more like getting a lay of the land. Putting feelers out, if you will. Besides, you wouldn't be their only distraction."

"Competition?"

"If you count the FBI as competition."

"So you're saying the field is hot at the moment?"

"I'm saying the field is wide open. The FBI has its hands full with the Albanians, so they won't be looking at anybody else. Not yet, at least."

There's a lengthy pause on the other end of the line. Bob—I've decided I'm going to call him Bob—is thinking it over.

"So that's it? You want us to make problems for the Capja in exchange for this alleged ledger?"

"Oh, no. You giving the Albanians a run for their money is just a bonus for me. What I want is a name."

Bob hesitates. There's a palpable tension on the other end of the line.

"Whose name?" he asks.

"Not a who. A what."

"What?"

A put the line on mute again and say to Sam, "would you mind?" Then I motion with my hand towards the window in the direction of our friend with the telephoto lens. He rolls his eyes at me, but takes my meaning and leaves to get details on the guy and his car. He can be tractable some of the time. It's why I keep him around.

"I need the name of the car rental agency La Linea used in LA ten years ago."

"What? Why?"

"It's—"

"Unrelated, yes, I gathered." Bob sighs heavily. "Fine. But it'll take me some time to dig through old records. I don't know it off the top of my head."

"Understandable," I reply smoothly. "We'll need to meet up so I can hand off the ledger anyway."

Murphy doesn't even blink, because Murphy is tractable pretty much all of the time. It's why I sent Sam for reconnaissance instead of Murphy. Sam would defi-nitely have objected to me setting up a tête-à-tête with yet another representative of a syndicate. And I just don't have time to defend every single little potentially deadly decision I make.

"Midnight. Torrence Auto Wreck—"

"I'm going to stop you right there," I say. I've had my fill of junkyards. "Meet me at the Chicken Shack in the UC Atrium in one hour."

"The Blackhawks are playing tonight. It'll be packed."

"That's the idea," I say. "I like my clandestine encounters with a dash of witness protection."

I mentally high-five myself for that improvised bit of prodding. If the cartel is responsible for the catfish, then my witness protection dig will add a layer of groundwork for when I drive the hammer home at our meetup.

"Fine," he mutters back. Then he disconnects the call.

"Bold of you," Murphy says from where he's tinkering with his new toy. "But if your end game is matching up the white Plymouth that supposedly hit Carmen with whoever rented it, there are a few holes in your plan. One, Carmen was theoretically killed *eight* years ago, not ten. Two, if she faked her death, it wouldn't have been the cartel that rented the Plymouth. Three, even if it was La Linea, they might not have rented the car at all—it might have belonged to someone who lived there. And four, did you say LA? Anton's family lives in Detroit."

"Semantics," I say, picking up my phone again and scrolling through my contacts.

"How is any of that semantics?"

I press a name and put the phone up to my ear again. "You got that mobile phone scanner set up yet?" I say as the other end of the line rings through.

"Yes..." he says. And then, "Oh..." as his eyes light up with understanding.

Meanwhile, on the other end of the phone line, a low and bitter voice says, "What?"

"Hi, there, Han, how're you doing?"

"You better be dying," she says with a barely concealed snarl.

"Not yet," I say brightly. "But I could be in an hour. Want to come watch?"

13

THE A.D.

United Center leading up to an NHL hockey game is every bit as chaotic as I expected. I've never been to a game myself. And technically, I'm not going to the hockey game now. I just need a highly public place I'm less likely to get murdered at.

So in I go, pushing open a glass door with more optimism than I deserve. Han is already inside and has cozied herself up in a spot with perfect line of sight to where Bob and I will be. Sam also insisted on coming, so he's at my six, no doubt looking as surly as he did when I told him about this plan. Murphy is in my ear, grumbling that he's hungry, and I'd better bring him some chicken this time.

The plan is to get Bob talking, give him something to chew on, then have Murphy tail him until he starts making phone calls. The beautiful thing about a mobile phone scanner is that Murphy should be able to hear both sides of any conversation made within range. If Murphy can catch a call relating to Carmen, or better yet, impersonating Carmen, then we'll obviously know the cartel is the catfish.

"Enough woolgathering, grifter. Pay attention," Han adds through my earpiece. I knew it was a mistake giving her access to my eardrums during a con.

Grudgingly, I scan our surroundings. The Atrium is a monstrosity of a building. Walls of glass and metal, at turns deflecting or invisible. Rather like grifters, to be honest.

Telephoto-lens dude is standing in the Madhouse Team store, pretending to peruse a rack of jerseys as we pass. With pitch black wraparound Ray-Bans and a matching horseshoe mustache, he looks the part of the thick-neck, low-acuity backup. I dismiss him as basically irrelevant.

We take the stairs to the second floor and locate the Chicken Shack wedged between a high-end bar for bigwigs and a carry-out convenience store. The Michael Jordan statue sits on the ground floor just below us, its gravity-defying basketball waiting to impale anyone foolish enough to jump the railing.

I sit on a pleather-covered bar stool welded to its neighbors and the table. Across from me, Bob is leaning indifferently against the stool. He's five-foot-nine, and looks like an extra from *Duck Dynasty*. He's also wearing sunglasses, Oakleys with a more classic style. The mottled brown beard hanging halfway to his navel and his camo trucker hat suggest that he gets the majority of his wardrobe from Preppers Supply Co. He's even wearing a tactical watch with a paracord band. Not the type I'd expect to be involved with a Mexican cartel.

A sea of people stream in two directions behind us, some making their way to the line for chicken, but most ferrying to or from the stadium. I'm not too worried about being overheard, and I doubt Bob is either.

"Hi, Bob," I say, offering my hand to shake. "I'm Julep."

He starts a bit, his shoulders tensing. "How'd you know my name was Bob?" he asks, sounding nervous and ignoring my hand.

I shrug and smile enigmatically. I'm tempted to tell him I was just using it as a placeholder, but it's better for me in this instance if he thinks I'm smarter than I am.

"Shall we get down to business?" I ask instead, taking a flash drive out of my pocket and laying it on the table between us.

He nods to a pencil pusher I hadn't noticed was waiting just off to the side. He shuffles forward, a slim silver laptop under his arm. With mussed and slightly greasy brown hair, big eyes, and even bigger hands and feet, he looks like I imagine Murphy would have looked if his fashion-forward girlfriend hadn't gotten hold of him.

Mr. Accountant sets the laptop on the table and flips it open, taking the flash drive and plugging it in. Sam looks like he's itching to explain to me what's happening, but I know enough by now to recognize an air-gapped setup when I see one.

The man taps through a few commands, opens a few files, and Bob's your uncle—er, so to speak. He nods a confirmation to Bob, who seems satisfied with the man's opinion on the matter, because Bob then turns back to me.

"Out of professional courtesy, can you tell me *why* you want the information about the rental agency we used in a completely different city in a completely different decade?"

"I cannot," I say, adding a touch of playful regret to my voice. "Confidentiality, you know."

He grunts at me but leans forward anyway, sliding a scrap of paper across the pretentious slab of wood serving as our table. I accept my prize with a smile, turning it over to read the name, and then handing the scrap to Sam without looking at him. Sam takes the scrap with a barely discernible eye-roll that I don't have to see to know is there. He knows I'm showing off, as if I'm a big, bad bigwig just like Bob.

"Thank you ever so much," I say with a saccharine expression. "Good doing business with you."

Then I slide off my stool, the hook just about planted. I take two steps and then turn and look casually over my shoulder.

"One more thing," I say. "Santiago says hi."

Sam shakes his head almost imperceptibly at me, as

I fall into step beside him. We rejoin the throng of hockey fans, standing out in our lack of Blackhawks gear, as they shift and press their way toward the stadium doors. We peel off at the stairs and start our descent.

Han meets us halfway, coming from the other side of the Atrium where she's been monitoring the interaction. Her hands are buried deep in her bomber jacket pockets. She's weaponless, due to having to walk through metal detectors to get in here, but she's a weapon herself, so she doesn't exactly look nervous. She has a nose ring I never noticed before. I try not to notice things about her that make her seem cool.

"Anything I should know?" I ask her, leaving the question intentionally vague. If I'm more specific she'll answer only exactly what I ask out of spite.

"Bob Jimenez. Recruiter. Not high up the chain but not low down either. Don't think he'd trade in bad faith, that's not his rep. But he's still cartel. If he thinks you're playing him, he'll kill you without thinking twice."

"I'm not playing him," I tell her, because I'm still not fully comfortable trusting her. And in any case, it's true. I'm not playing him—I'm just spying on him. "I gave him the goods and told him the truth. Santiago does say hi. Well, a Santiago descendent says hi, anyway."

"Somehow I don't see him as a person that splits hairs quite as finely as you do," Sam says, his tone disapproving. "Do you think he'll bite?"

"If the cartel is behind the catfishing, he'll immediately make the connection and start making calls."

"Assuming he's involved."

"He's in Chicago. Juarez doesn't have much of a presence here, hence the ledger bait. If he's here, and Carmen is supposedly here, it's a good bet he's involved, or at least knows enough to perk up at a weird comment like 'Santiago says hi.' All we need is for him to make one call."

"And then what?" Han asks. "Not that I care beyond keeping my promise to keep you alive. But how exactly do you plan to stop the Juarez cartel from doing whatever the hell they want?"

"The same way I plan on making that ledger I gave them as toxic to them as it is to the Albanians."

"You're going to tell Mike to have the FBI take them out," Sam says with a sigh. "I don't think Mike is going to be happy you added another syndicate to his already overflowing plate."

"He'll be happy when he gets commendations and promotions and stuff. Don't worry about the lawmen, Sam. They can take care of themselves. Far better than the Anton Walkers of the world can, anyway."

He nods his head to concede the point as we push through the glass doors and back out into the October night. I pull my jacket closer around me, wishing I still had Dani's jacket. But I don't. And I may not ever again, if I don't find her soon. I try not to dwell on it, but I feel the familiar pit opening up in my stomach. I swallow hard.

Then Murphy snarks in my ear, "Don't tell me you didn't get any chicken. I'm freaking starving."

I smile, a rising fondness for my minions warming my ribcage. Sometimes they're so predictably adorable at just the right time.

"You're up, Murphy," I say. "Catch us a catfish."

SAM DROPS me off at home, which is nice, as taking the 'L' would have been easily twice as long a journey. I don't mind riding the 'L' most days, but I'm dog tired tonight. It's not even ten yet, and I feel like I've lived three lifetimes. I'd blame it on the fact that the junkyard incident was just the night before, and I haven't been getting very much sleep the past few months, but the truth is, I struggle with energy and motivation a lot lately. When I'm not manically obsessing about finding Dani, I'm exhausted. Adrenal overload. I saw a video on YouTube about it.

"You're home early," Angela says from the dining room, where she's set up her sewing machine to make herself a dress. She's wearing reading glasses with a sparkly chain attached to both temples.

I drop my bag and coat near the door and walk to the table to admire her handiwork.

"It's looking great," I say truthfully. I may have to conscript her for disguise making.

"Thanks," she says, adjusting a couple of pins near the edge. "It's a simple pattern, so it should come together in time for the banquet."

The local FBI office, Mike's office, holds an annual fundraiser banquet every year, and every year, Angela makes herself a new dress for it. Another few years, and she might be able to open her own boutique.

"You want anything?" I ask as I head to the kitchen. That Orange Julius seems like a million years ago now.

"Tea, please," she says.

I make a face. Tea. Gross. But I dutifully break out the kettle and loose leaf. At least I know how to brew tea now, thanks to Angela's tutelage. And, hey, it could come in handy someday, if I'm ever called upon to impersonate a character from *Downton Abbey*.

The front door opens again, admitting a whirlwind of Mike energy.

"Listen, McTaverty, I know it's a madhouse in there, but you can't just let them kill each other. Use the interrogation rooms to separate them if you have to. And finish processing the fingerprints for Block D while you're at it. I'll log in from home."

With an exasperated huff, Mike ends the call and pockets his phone.

"Rough day at the office?" Angela asks, turning her face up for a kiss.

Mike dutifully bends down and lands a peck somewhere nearish her lips.

"You can say that again," he says in his blustery voice, as he deposits his briefcase on the table across from Angela's sewing machine. "*Someone* decided it was a nifty idea to stir up the Albanians, and now the holding cells are filled with two types of gangsters: the ones who, of course, have never done anything criminal and wouldn't talk even if they had, and the ones who insist they'll spill everything the minute you give them a pen. We're barely keeping them from murdering each other."

I manage to smother a snort of satisfaction. The MCC and I have history, and I can't say I'm not a little smug that they're going through a rough patch, thanks to me. I take the tea ball out of Angela's tea and hand her the mug.

"Thanks," she says with a tired smile and takes a sip. "Albanians, huh?"

"Albanians," Mike echoes, sounding disgusted.

"I may have some good news on that front," I say, choosing my words carefully as I slide into the seat next to the one he's just sat down in.

"Oh, really?" he asks doubtfully.

"You may not to have to worry about the Albanians turning on each other, once you start adding members of the Juarez cartel to the mix. They'll be too busy trying to kill the rival syndicate to fight among themselves."

Mike lowers his head into his hands. "Tell me," he says in a defeated voice.

So I do, highlighting as many of the good points as I can.

"And they have the ledger now?"

"Yep. You're welcome," I add with a smirk. Sometimes I can't help myself.

"God, I miss Dani," Mike says, then immediately throws me an apologetic look. The lurch in my internal organs notwithstanding, his instant contrition at reminding me of my loss mellows out his consternation with me, so I can't really complain. Much.

"S'all right, G-man. I'm not likely to break. Which is apparently something I keep having to say whenever little incidents like this crop up." I snag an apple from the bowl in the middle of the table and take a bite.

"I still don't understand why you felt you had to actively reach out to La Linea. As if my hands aren't already full enough, thank you very much."

"It's for the catfishing case," I say, around my bite of apple. "Murphy's finding out if they're involved."

"And how's he doing that?" Mike asks suspiciously.

"A grifter never reveals her secrets," I say with a waggle of fingers. "But he's a safe distance away, and in any case, I have something else to discuss with you."

"What's that?" he asks, still suspicious. I honestly don't know why he doesn't trust me by now.

I take another bite of apple, pausing for effect.

"You ever heard of a company called Brillion?"

THE NEXT DAY, I skip the last period—track and field, ugh—and stroll over to the Ballou to get a jump start on Murphy's report, which he texted me that he'd left on my desk. But when I let myself into J.D. & Associates, it isn't empty.

"Who the hell are you?" I ask, stopping short a bare foot into my own office.

The man leaning a hip against my desk, Murphy's report flipped open in his hands, has a lean runner's build and a blue suit that fits him like a glove. His haircut is so painfully trendy that it'll be cringey in less time than it takes to grow out. But he exudes a confidence, earned or not, that reeks of badge.

"Pardon the intrusion," the man says, his voice oilier than his hair product. He pushes himself upright, away from my desk, and extends his hand. At first, I interpret that as an offer to shake, but then I notice the wallet he's slipped out of a pants pocket.

"Chief Deputy United States Marshal Daniel Curran," he says, flipping the wallet open to show me the badge. It looks legit enough—circle, star, eagle flattened like roadkill in the center. But credentials are easy to fake, as any good grifter can tell you. I'm pretty sure I have my own U.S. Marshal badge stashed somewhere under a loose floorboard.

"What do you want?"

He holds up Murphy's report. "Group project? Seems like this kid Murphy is doing the heavy lifting."

My heart thumps. "Why does that sound like a threat?"

"Why would it be a threat? You're not doing anything illegal, are you?" he says with a smile so greasy you could fry eggs in it.

"We're investigators." I raise my chin in spite of myself. Who does this glorified pencil pusher think he is?

"You're children." His smile turns acidic. "And you're going to get hurt."

Another threat. Whoever this guy is, he's got my hackles up to my ears. I stuff my hands in my pockets, one curled around my phone, the other around my house keys. I really need to start carrying some kind of bear spray.

"What do you want?" I ask again. "And don't say *your help*, because you've definitely lost your shot at that."

He laughs. "I wouldn't dream of it. In fact, I'm here to help you."

Damn cops. They're all the worst. Except Mike. Well, mostly Mike. He can also be the worst, come to think of it.

"Let me save you some trouble then—I didn't ask for your help."

"Whether you asked or not you need it," he says, tossing Murphy's report back onto my desk as if it were garbage. "You're barking up a dangerous tree, and it's not even the right one. Your *associate's* report will tell you as much."

"What do you know about it?"

"I know that Carmen Walker is alive."

I glare at him, grinding my molars into dust.

He leans closer into my personal space. Another inch, and that aquiline nose is going to get punched.

"I happen to know she's alive," he continues, lowering his voice. "Because I'm the one who brought her into WITSEC."

He takes a step back and gives me a "sorry, kid" rueful smile that doesn't reach his eyes. Then he takes his leave, whistling as he shuts the door behind him.

"Jerk," I say to his no-longer-present self.

I'm not mad because he was about as condescending through that whole exchange as a comics bro bemoaning the explicitly diverse casting of all the new Marvel movies. I mean, yes, that, too. But if I'm honest, I'm more mad because there's a very good chance he's not lying.

14

THE CALL

"Thanks, Anton," I say, as I wrap up the call. "I know it's not what you were expecting."

I hang up and place the handset of my office phone back in the cradle.

"He seemed to take it okay?" Lily says, her voice tilting up at the end as if it were more of a question than a statement.

I shrug. "I mean, her being alive is a good thing. But it's gotta be hard reconciling reality with your gut's misgivings. I know a thing or two about that."

Lily nods, returning to her homework. I'm pretty sure she's doodling in her spiral rather than factoring equations, but I'm not one to judge.

I pick up a pen to make a note on Murphy's report, and put the end of it in my mouth to chew on it, thinking. It's been an hour since Chief Deputy Curran came, dropped his bomb, and left. St. Aggie's is out now, and Lily's come straight here after last period to wait for our ride back across town with Mike. Sam, Murphy, and Bryn are at some nerdy after-school club—robotics, I think?—and Dani is... well. In the wind. So it's just me and Lil.

Curran was right about one thing, I was barking up the wrong tree, according to Murphy's report. Bob did make a call that night about my Santiago remark, but it was clear that neither he nor whoever he was talking to had a clue what it meant. The name Carmen didn't come up even once.

I write an asterisk beside a few parts that I'll want to include in my overall report to Anton, then I throw the pen on the desk.

Something doesn't feel right about this. After Curran left, I called the local marshal's office and asked to be transferred to Curran's office. No answer, which, frankly, I expected. But I got his voicemail, which clearly stated his name and rank and to leave a message with the operator or call 911 in the event of an emergency. I hung up, frustrated.

If Curran is real, then he's likely telling the truth. But why would he tell me? No marshal worth his salt would ever confirm to a civilian that a witness was in the program. And if he knew she was contacting her family, he'd put a stop to it, wouldn't he? Why go out of his way to get me to back off? I don't buy for a second it's to save me from the mob.

I reach for the landline phone again to call Anton. But before I get so much as a finger on the handset, my cell nearly vibrates itself off my desk. The Caller ID says *Anton*.

I answer and say, "I was just about to..."

"She called. She's on the other line," Anton interrupts me. "I told her dad was on call-waiting. What do I do?"

"Merge the calls," I tell him. Then I put my phone on mute and turn to Lily. "Get Murphy in here now."

She jumps up instantly, for once not rolling her eyes or dragging her feet. She must have heard my mess-with-me-at-your-peril tone.

"...day at school?" I hear the catfish ask as Anton merges the calls.

Anton answers with some inane details about soccer practice while I scramble for my earbuds and pop them in my ears. I tap a finger impatiently until they connect with my phone, hoping he draws out his story until I'm back in the game. When the sound clicks back on, I swipe to my text messages and frantically start typing to Anton.

Ask her what happened that night.

He thumbs-ups my message.

"Hey, mom," he says, hesitating as if coming up with a way to broach a delicate subject. "I know you don't like to talk about it, but can you tell me what happened that night? I just... I need to know."

"I told you, baby, it's all behind us."

"It's just—were you hurt? Did you know it was coming?"

He does such a good job of sounding worried and vulnerable that I want to give him an Oscar. This boy has potential.

"Oh, sweetie, I wasn't hurt. I was told what would happen."

She never called me sweetie, he taps back to me.

"Why couldn't you take us with you?" he says to her.

I wince.

Get back to that night. We need details.

Pushing emotionally has its place in the grifter toolbox, but not in this case. If she is an impostor, pushing the emotional aspects will only spook her into changing the subject or hanging up altogether. We need to catch her in a lie, not a murder. Unless the person on the phone *is* Carmen's murderer.

Murphy bursts in through the door, followed quickly by Bryn, Sam, and Lily.

"I couldn't take you away from school, from your friends, the rest of the family. I wanted you to be safe, but I also wanted you to be happy."

I nearly gag from the whine in her tone. When did AI get the sappiness upgrade? Gross.

I gesture to Murphy to set up the recording. Not that the gestures themselves make much sense, I imagine. But he catches on regardless and opens his own phone to an app he's been developing that will record a conversation without letting the other party (or parties) know that the call is being recorded. It's illegal, but it's not like that's ever stopped us before. At his nod, I merge him into the now four-way phone call.

"I get that you needed to protect us," Anton says. "But I'm not a kid anymore. What happened that night?"

I hear this both in my earbuds and also out loud in the room. Murphy must have put his phone on speaker so that Lily, Sam, and Bryn could listen in as well. He'd better have remembered to put his phone on mute.

"I'm not supposed to talk about it, Anton. Why are you so insistent about this?"

Therapist, I type at light speed and send.

There's a pause on Anton's end. I will him to understand my vague direction.

"I have this therapist," he says at last. There's doubt in his voice, but he's on the right track. Now if he can just sell it. "And he says that if I know more about what happened that night, I can put it behind me. Closure, or something."

Okay? he sends back.

I send him a clapping emoji.

"Well...all right," the impostor says hesitantly "I stumbled upon something I shouldn't have. And I really can't tell you about that, so don't ask."

"That's all right," he assures her. "Go on."

"I saw something I shouldn't have. I didn't know what to do, so I went to the police."

"And they helped you?"

"They called in the FBI. Because of...who was involved."

That perks my ears up. If the FBI helped her, then they have a file on her. And if they have a file on her, then Mike can dig it up for me.

"And the FBI staged everything?"

"Yes," she says, and I grin. Finally, a break. I'm just texting that I've got what I need for now, when she continues. "Listen, Anton..." I stop texting mid-word, my grifter senses on high alert. Something's up. Something big.

"Yeah?" he prompts her, clearly trying to rein in his impatience at her hesitation.

"I can't say much or he'll find out. But there's something I have to do. One thing, and I can come home."

"What?" Anton says, sounding as mind blown as I feel.

"I have to go," she says suddenly and ends the call abruptly.

"Hello?" Anton asks, his voice breaking.

"Julep?" Sam asks gently, nudging me out of my shock. I slowly rise to my feet, blinking a few times to reorient myself to this new information. I make a cutting gesture at Murphy, and he dutifully drops the line, ending the recording.

I unmute my line. "Anton? You okay?"

He swallows hard on the other end of the line and clears his throat. I can see him in my mind's eye, rubbing the heel of his hand across one of his eyes, ordering back any errant tears. Poor kid.

"Yeah," he says finally. "What the hell could she...? Was I wrong? Is she actually...?"

"I don't know," I say with steel in my voice. "But I intend to find out."

"Hey, Mike," Lily says as she beats me to the front seat of Mike's Honda. "Tell us you got something from that Detroit PD contact."

"Hey, that's my line," I grouse as I clamber into the backseat.

"I was the one who asked him to look into it," Lily points out. "So?" she says to Mike.

He sighs heavily, and hands Lily a large brown envelope. "Just came by courier this afternoon. I told you, Deanna's not homicide, so neither of you ever saw this, you got me?"

"You got it, boss," I say with a mock salute and lean forward between their bucket seats so I can read over Lily's shoulder.

"Seatbelt!" Mike says with an irritated glance at me in the rearview.

"It's on, G-man," I snipe back, tapping the strap nearly strangling me with its death grip.

He grumbles something uncomplimentary as he exits onto the 290.

A hush settles over the car interior as Lily and I read

through the admittedly thin report. The first page covers the demographics, the incident, the officers on the scene. The next two pages are a copy of the death certificate and the coroner's report with a big red HOMICIDE stamped in block letters across the top section.

The coroner's report is what you'd expect—death by blunt force trauma from collision with a car, speed determined by injuries to be in the range of 30 to 40 miles per hour. The injury most likely responsible for death was to the back of her head, where it was surmised that she bounced off the pavement after being hit.

The following page is a photocopy of a series of graphic coroner's images helpfully cataloging the injuries, complete with rulers and notations to provide additional details. Lily makes a distressed sound and pushes the folder at me, looking out the window to compose herself.

I lean back, taking the folder with me to get it out of Lily's line of sight. It's not a bullet wound, but I have no doubt that she's thinking about her brother right now. For the millionth time, I feel like a monster for getting him killed. But I can't do anything about that now. What I can do is help Anton. I flip the page again to read through the final conclusion of the officer in charge of the case. Nothing particularly revelatory until I get to the officer's signature.

Daniel Curran.

That bastard. He wasn't the marshal who got her into WITSEC. He was the police officer who handled her supposed homicide. What if he wasn't lying about her being alive? What if he was lying about being her handler? What if what Carmen saw had to do with crooked cops, including Curran, and the FBI had to fake her death so that they could protect her from retribution from the very people who were supposed to help her? What if he then transferred to the marshals because he suspected she was still alive? What if he was trying to *find* her? If the FBI hid her, then maybe they'd know who her real handler is. Which reminds me…

"Mike," I snap suddenly, slamming the folder closed and launching myself to the space between the seats again. Mike swerves, cursing in surprise.

"Julep, what the heck? Sit back, will you?"

"I need you to look up Carmen Walker's case."

"I did," he says, gesturing to the file I'm holding in my hand.

"Not the PD case, the FBI case," I say. "The impersonator, or whoever she is, claims that the FBI helped relocate her when she faked her death. There must be a file on her if she's telling the truth."

Mike snorts. "Any other rules I can break for you while I'm at it?"

"As a matter of fact…"

"No, I'm not putting an illegal wiretap on Curran's phone."

"Well, it was worth a shot."

"I can't believe I agreed to this," Han mutters as she puts the binoculars to her eyes.

We're sitting under a small copse of trees next to an almost empty parking lot outside the local U.S. Marshals office. The area is well lit, at least. Not like certain junkyards which shall remain nameless.

"Could be worse," I say, huddling into my coat to protect my exposed neck from the wind.

"How so? I'd dearly love to know," she says, lowering the binoculars since it's painfully obvious there's nothing to see yet.

"You could be here with me *and* Dani."

I really don't know why I keep poking her sore spots. It's not fair. And she did save my bacon from the Albanians. It must be my basic operating system of evilness. It's decided she's the enemy, and I must therefore take no prisoners.

But rather than the scathing look of hatred I expect her to turn on me, she gives me an assessing look instead.

"Actually, I'd rather that than know she's with Petrov."

A chill of dread suffuses my entire being. She must know something.

"What happened?" I ask. And this time, I don't mean *why didn't she come to me instead of you?* This time I mean, *what happened to her? What happened to you?*

She must hear the difference in my voice, the unusual note of humility, because she answers.

"I got in a tight spot trying to rescue some kidnapped kids," she says simply. "Dani got us out. All of us. Except herself."

I swallow hard, fighting back a wave of nausea and fear and grief so strong I almost break down. In front of Han. Unacceptable.

"She's all right, though? The kids? You're all okay?"

"Yes," Han says softly. "They let her go eventually. But she had to go back to *him*."

The way she spat the word does not give me a lot of confidence that Petrov is treating Dani as a valued member of his team.

"How do we get her back, Han?" I ask, surprising myself with the vulnerability in the question. When did I start showing this woman my tender underbelly?

"We don't," Han said, her voice cracking. "She'll come back when she can."

"What if she never can?"

Han returns to the binoculars without a word, giving me my answer. As it happens, it's not an answer I can accept.

"Heads up, grifter," she says suddenly, handing me the binoculars. "Movement at the side door."

I adjust the lenses slightly to fit my gaze, and Chief Douchebag United States Marshal Daniel Curran comes into focus. He's setting his briefcase down to pull out his phone and make a call.

"Him?" she asks.

"Yep," I confirm, handing her back the binoculars.

She peers through them again, adjusting her position slightly.

"I don't recognize him," she says. "If he's syndicate, he's buried. Or he's just somebody I've never met before. You had to know this was a long shot."

"That he'd have obvious ties to a criminal organization? Sure. But that's not why I asked you to come."

She frowns, shifting away from me as if prepping for a fight. Which is hilarious, her thinking I'm some kind of threat.

"I miss her," I admit finally without looking at Han, tucking my wind-stung hands under my arms. "You're the only one who gets it. You're the only one who misses her even half as much as I do."

Han grunts. Then puts the binoculars up to her eyes again.

15

THE FIELD TRIP

I t's oh-dark-thirty. The Ballou has just opened. And I've already been here for an hour, staring at this jenky whiteboard. I've told Yaji, now that he's officially on duty, to bring me another latte every hour on the hour until I tell him to stop, but I fear it's going to take more than a little thinking juice to get my brain wrestled into submission.

"Look, it's not personal," I say to the whiteboard. "It's just you ruin the entire aesthetic, you know what I mean?"

My phone buzzes. It's Mike asking where I am. I text him a pin of my location so he won't worry. Mike sends me a thumbs up, and I remind him to look into the Walker file for me. He sends another thumbs up, and I pocket my phone again.

The board has mostly pictures and notecards with a few black dry-erase lines linking them together. I pick up a red marker and start filling in the white space with questions.

At the top middle of the whiteboard is a notecard with Carmen Walker's name, a giant question mark, and the words 'teacher,' 'death by hit and run,' and 'cartel daughter.'

Branching off from that notecard on one side is a notecard reading 'Juarez Cartel/La Linea' and a grainy picture of Bob Jimenez from Murphy's camera phone taken from a distance and zoomed in affixed to the bottom left corner. I draw a large red X to the left of the notecard, the cartel having been more or less ruled out for now.

Branching off from Carmen on the other side is a notecard with the word 'WITSEC' on it. A professional photo of Daniel Curran that Murphy printed from the internet is attached to the WITSEC card. Next to the WITSEC card, I write 'FBI?' Hopefully, we'll have something from Mike before the day is out to confirm or deny that assertion from the catfish. Then next to the picture of Curran, I write 'DPD' for Detroit Police Department.

Someone, probably Murphy, added notecards below Curran's photo, one saying 'AD?' and the other saying 'syndicate?' I put an X next to syndicate. Han didn't recognize him. And even though the absence of intel on that front doesn't explicitly rule out that he's affiliated with one of the crime families, my gut tells me that isn't what Curran is about. He's shady, but he doesn't have a syndicate vibe. Plus, it doesn't really matter who he's affiliated with if he's the one leading the charge on the catfishing.

So that leaves the AD branch.

I take a step back and look at the board as a whole. What am I missing?

I move back to the board and uncap the marker. Then I draw two lines under the AD, one leading to the word 'LYING' and the other leading to 'TELLING THE TRUTH.' I cap the marker again, lost in thought. If he's telling the truth, and Carmen is still alive, then what is the one thing she has to do to come home? And why put her at risk like that anyway? Is he using her as bait? That's hardly normal WITSEC procedure. He's going rogue, if that's the case. Adding further to this point is the fact that he told me about Carmen in the first place. No U.S. Marshal in good standing and with any kind of ethical boundaries would tell a complete, unrelated stranger that one of their charges was in witness protection. It made no sense.

So then the logical conclusion is that he's lying. But lying about what, exactly? And why? If he's telling the truth about Carmen being alive but lying about his involvement with her because he's actually trying to track her down, then he's a danger to Anton's whole family. If he's lying about Carmen being alive, then why have the impostor claim she can come home?

Then it hits me all at once. I cast my gaze up to Carmen's card again, or, more importantly, to the empty white space beside it. There's a card that should be there that's missing.

I grab my phone from my pocket and speed dial Han's phone number.

"What?" comes a sleepy, surly voice over the line.

My heartbeat picks up as the con tumbles into my head. I need to make this quick, or everyone will be in danger.

"How fast can you get us to Detroit?"

YOU MAY BE WONDERING why I didn't ask Sam to drive me. Or Murphy. Or even Mike. The answers are simple. Mike wouldn't let me get within five miles of anything potentially dangerous, especially not after everything I've put him through with the Albanians and La Linea, not to mention everything else over the past year. Murphy's van Bessie is a fossil of an automobile and can barely manage the speed limit most days, let alone high-octane driving. And Sam... I would sooner let the bad guys win than let Sam anywhere near the crosshairs of a U.S. Marshal. He's already been detained by the FBI because of me, and has just recently gotten out of another dust-up with the FBI over a bank robbery. The last thing he needs is the marshals on his case as well.

Thus, I find myself clinging like a desperate and terrified barnacle to Han's back as she darts in and out of speeding traffic along the freeway connecting Chicago and Detroit. Luckily, it's so cold that I can barely think about anything else. I feel the terror clutching my heart, but the cold of the wind streaming around us at this breakneck speed has slowed its frantic beating to its normal pace.

I've buried my face in Han's back, attempting to shrink behind her body while still clinging on for dear life. I have decided to walk back to Chicago rather than attempt this nearly four-hour whiplash through Antarctica a second time.

My face is numb and my bones chattering as much as my teeth when we pull into a gas station and finally roll to a stop. I stumble off the bike, my legs barely able to hold me up. I may never walk a straight line again.

I hear a snort behind me, and I'm so out of it that I can't even spare a scathing glance at my torturer/driver. I push my way into the attached convenience store and hobble to the bathroom at the back. I huddle over the sink, splashing lukewarm water on my face just to feel something.

My phone rings, and I ignore it. I opt instead to do something with the hair that's either been matted to my head by the helmet or bushed out by the wind, despite the braid I tied it into. I didn't think to bring a brush—rookie move on my part—but I do a fair enough job with my fingers to at least fashion it into a messy bun.

My phone rings again. I fish it out of my pocket and

lay it on the cleanest part of the sink rim I can find, silencing the ringer. Then I shimmy out of my road clothes and into my disguise, trademark glasses and all.

My phone rings again, and this time I answer.

"You have two minutes," I say, having no idea who's on the other end. I pull tubes of concealer and mascara out of my bag, just to even out the wreckage the motorcycle ride made of my face.

"Why are you in Detroit?" Sam asks, his voice nearly as stern as Mike's usually is when I do something less than prudent.

"Why are you spying on me?" I shoot back. I find it's better to respond to a question you don't want to answer with another question.

"Because you missed our scheduled meetup at ten."

Oh.

"I forgot about that."

"No doubt because you're distracted by being in Detroit. Why are you in Detroit?"

He knows my evasion tactics too well, dang it.

"I'm in Detroit because of the whiteboard."

"The whiteboard forced you to go to Detroit? Without telling anyone where you were going or why?"

"I told someone," I say defensively. "Han knows exactly where I am."

"Great. And how many of us have Han's phone number? How many of our phone numbers does Han have? I can tell you, in case you don't happen to know. It's zero. Zero numbers, Julep."

"Well... I can rectify that."

Sam makes a noise like I'm actively strangling his last nerve.

"I'm not doing anything dangerous, Sam. I mean, I'm pretty sure it's not dangerous. At least sixty percent sure. That's a decent amount, given my track record."

"This isn't a joke, Julep. I know it's not a joke, because I'm not laughing. And neither is Mike."

"You told Mike?" I say, wounded by his nonchalant admission of betrayal. "You bonded way too much over that whole bank robbery thing."

There's a shuffling sound on the other end of the line, and the phone changes hands.

"There's no FBI file, Julep," Mike says into Sam's phone. "There's no Carmen Santiago Walker from Detroit in our database."

"You're sure?" But it's a ridiculous question. Of course he's sure. "Would the FBI have scrubbed the file when she entered WITSEC?"

"Not likely," Mike says. "It's not as if the FBI hides information from itself on the off chance its records will eventually be hacked."

Well, that information makes things more interesting. Either someone cared enough about Carmen to hide her involvement with the FBI, or the impostor was lying about the FBI being part of her disappearance. I'm betting on the latter, given that Curran seems to be the only person in law enforcement still connected to Carmen. He was never affiliated with the FBI, so he couldn't have erased her file from the FBI database.

Another scuffle for the phone, and Sam is back on the line.

"What are you planning on doing? We don't have enough information to pull off a credible con yet."

"I told you. The whiteboard pointed me in the right direction, though I'm kicking myself for not seeing it sooner. Don't tell Murphy. He'll be insufferable about it."

"Julep..." Sam says, his voice dipping low into warning. "Don't do anything that Mike will have to clean up when we get there."

"That's four hours from now," I say, keeping my tone light. "What could possibly happen in four hours?"

Then I hang up before he can start listing all the trouble I've gotten myself into in fewer than thirty minutes. I swear, ever since he ran his own con at military school, he acts like he's the boss of me. It's still my PI firm, for Pete's sake.

"Grifter, are you coming or what?"

I hastily straighten my outfit, take one final glance in the mirror, decide that it'll have to do, and then stride out to meet Han in the chip aisle.

"You sure about this?" she says, eyebrow raised.

"Of course."

She gestures for me to precede her. We leave the store

and hoof it through two side-by-side parking lots to get from the gas station to the liquor store where Anton's dad works.

If you're lost, let me catch you up. What I figured out at the Ballou was that I don't need to know whether Carmen Walker is actually dead or alive. What I need to know is *what does Anton's father have that Curran wants.* Anton's father is the mark, after all, not Anton's mother. So what does George Walker know? Did Carmen give him something incriminating? Did she somehow implicate Curran in some sort of cover up? Because if the catfish is lying about who she is, then she just gave Anton the biggest shutout ever, which he no doubt passed on to his dad— *one thing, and I can come home.*

When we get to the store, Han opens the door for me. Anton's dad is sitting behind the cash register when I enter, scrolling on his phone. I know it's him from his Facebook photo, and from his name tag, which reads *George Walker.* Still looks young for having fathered five kids, though his shoulders have a stoop to them and his face has lines that usually come with greater age.

He looks up from his Samsung as I approach the counter.

"Can I help you?" he asks, a pleasant smile in place. He has kind eyes. I wouldn't peg him for someone who'd be involved in something nefarious. But who knows? People do all kinds of things for all kinds of reasons.

"I'd like to ask you a few questions, if I may," I say,

pulling out my wallet, and flashing him my fake credentials—press credentials, that is, for the Colby High School newspaper. "We're doing a tribute to Anton's mother for a special edition of our school newspaper."

He blinks in surprise. "Why?"

"Anton's winning an award for an essay he wrote about her. Did he not tell you? Sorry if I spoiled the surprise. But we kind of need some background information for the piece on her that goes with the story about Anton winning the contest."

"That's...wow. He didn't mention it." George taps the counter thoughtfully, absorbing the news. "What kind of information are you looking for?"

"Just some basic fact checking. For instance, how did you and Mrs. Walker meet?" I ask with a disarming smile. Starting with a softball question should help warm him up. I take a pen from behind my ear and note pad from my bag, and look at him expectantly.

"We met through our parents. Our fathers worked in the same business but for different companies. They had meetings now and then, and I'd tag along. Carmen and I were both kind of the black sheep of our families, so we hit it off right away. She was such a spitfire, with a streak of justice a mile wide."

His lips quirk up at the memory, a melancholy cast to his face as he sinks into the past.

"What business did you say your fathers were in?" I ask, trying not to sound too interested. "Readers like details," I add, trying to sound as awkward as a teenage journalist would in this situation.

"It doesn't matter now," he replies shaking his head. "Both our dads are long gone. But it was a bit of a Romeo and Juliet thing at the time. Neither of our families wanted us together."

"Why not?"

George shrugs. "Just different worlds. No good reason. Anyway, their objections obviously didn't mean much in the end. Carmen and I went our own way."

"That's beautiful, Mr. W," I say, scribbling illegible nonsense on my notepad. "And Mrs. W was a teacher at Dearborn Elementary, correct?"

"Yes. She wanted to teach where our children went to school…"

I nod, only half listening as he goes on about Carmen's teaching career. George's father being in the same profession as Carmen's could only mean one thing—his dad was cartel, too. Not the same cartel, but some sort of criminal syndicate with ties to La Linea.

Which then begs the question: what if George isn't the mark after all? What if he's a suspect?

My inner Mike is grounding me for a month over the mere possibility. Not only would I be in considerably more danger if George were somehow involved in killing Carmen, but I'd also be directly interfering in a criminal investigation. Which would not look so good on my probation report. I try not to let the chagrin show on my face. But in my defense, why would a WITSEC director be investigating a murder? It's way outside his jurisdiction. Besides, he told me Carmen was alive, not that he was investigating her death.

Meanwhile, my inner grifter is like, well, you're here now—might as well get the goods while you can.

"Where was Carmen going the night she died?" I ask, dropping the pretense of teen reporter and setting my notepad and pencil on the counter. "It was late for a school night, wasn't it? Why did she leave?"

George rubs a hand through his dark, close-cropped coils. "She never said. She just left. Do you really need this for your article?"

"She never said anything? Even something that didn't seem odd at the time? Like, 'I'm going to get milk'?"

He shakes his head, but then stops. "She didn't tell me she was leaving. But earlier that day she mentioned she'd had a difficult conversation with a student, and she needed to tell someone about it. I don't think it's connected, though. I got the impression she meant the principal, who wouldn't have been meeting with her at nine o'clock at night."

"Did you mention that to the police eight years ago?" I ask.

"No. Her death was an accident, so no one really asked."

"Do you know which student she was talking about?"

George's eyes narrow. "This isn't for any school newspaper article. Who are you really, and why are you asking me this?"

Funny story...you're being catfished by your dead wife and your son hired me to expose her.

I open my mouth but am saved having to answer as George himself is distracted by something outside the window.

"Trent?" he says, confused.

I turn just in time to see the gun.

16

THE SEAL

"Trent...?" George says again.

But the gunman doesn't answer, he just shoots.

Bottles of top-shelf liquor on the wall behind George explode in a fountain of glass and booze. I'm immediately thrown back in time four months, the image of myself and Lily huddling under a table in Bar63 while Spade opens fire on Joseph and Aadila clouding my brain. I shake my head hard, snapping myself back to the present.

"Stay down!" Han yells, and I dimly see her in my peripheral vision, pulling her own weapon.

Why is this happening? My head is thick with spider webs trapping every thought as I try to come up with a way out of this.

"Who the hell are you?" Trent shouts, twisting toward the new threat.

"Drop the weapon, and you'll never have to find out," Han shouts back.

He levels his pistol at her, and takes a shot, but she ducks behind some boxes and, presumably, scuttles further down the aisle out of the path of the bullet. Trent takes advantage of her losing line of sight and ducks behind his own barricade. Great. Now I'm back in the warehouse with Petrov's men, waiting for the FBI to save us. I have way too much drama in my life.

I drop to my knees and crawl behind the counter to check on George. He's bleeding from a wound in his shoulder, which looks more like a graze than a through-and-through. Ugh, I shouldn't have to know what those terms mean.

My own barely healed shoulder aches in sympathy as I grab a hand towel from the shelf under the cash register and press it against George's shoulder to staunch the bleeding.

I unlock my phone and dial 911. In the background I can hear the sharp firestorm of Han and Trent trading bullets back and forth.

"Who the hell's that?" I ask George as I will the call to connect.

"Old friend. Haven't seen him in years."

"Any idea why he wants to shoot you?"

"Thought he was trying to shoot you."

I have to acknowledge that George could be right. Lots of people get their kicks taking potshots at me. But in this case, it's much more likely he's here for George. If he were here for me, he wouldn't have been surprised by Han. Not to mention, George knows who he is, and I wouldn't know him from Adam. No one from Detroit wants me dead. Yet. That I know of.

"911, what's your emergency?" the operator prompts me once they connect to my call.

"Active shooter at Dearborn Liquor Emporium on Hubbard. Cashier shot."

I lower the phone and turn back to George. "Could it have to do with Carmen? Could Trent be trying to silence you from saying something you shouldn't?"

The operator interrupts tinnily through the phone speaker: "Are you safe? Is the shooter still there?"

I put the phone back to my ear. "For the moment, and yes."

George shakes his head, his lips pale and bloodless. "He was in the gang with me. My father. His father. But he went straight. Like me."

"Doesn't look like he stayed that way," I say.

The operator breaks in again. "I'm sending units now. ETA ten minutes. Can you get out?"

"No," I admit.

George gasps as I press the towel harder to his shoulder.

"I'll stay on the line with you until—"

I end the call. They have what they need, and I need to focus if I'm going to get us out of this.

"What's Trent do?" I ask George.

George answers through gritted teeth. "Cop."

"What?" I ask, ice skating down my spine.

"He's...a cop."

He's a cop. As in, Detroit Police Department, the same police department that may have covered up Carmen's murder. As in, the police department that is on its way here now. What's the likelihood that any of them will pick our side over his?

Crap. I should *not* have called 911.

I have to get Han the hell out of here. And George. And me. Mike is still hours away. Sam is going to *kill* me.

"Is there a back door?"

George shakes his head. "Employee stockroom. No door."

I scan the room for a way out. Fortunately, Han is between Trent and the front door. She could probably escape if she wanted to. *Un*fortunately, George and I are huddled behind the cash counter, which opens up to the middle of the room. He and I would have to crawl through the firefight in order to escape.

"Get out of here, Han!" I shout over the counter.

"If I go, he'll kill you!"

"If you don't, the cops will arrest you!"

Han swears a blue streak and shifts position. She doesn't leave.

That's when I see it. The basket of lighters next to the cash register. I'll have to pop up into Trent's line of sight to grab one. Only for a second, but I'll have to pick that second wisely.

He takes another shot, and Han responds in kind. As soon as I hear the retort from her gun, I pop up and snag a lighter, knocking the basket and the rest of its contents on the floor in my haste. I hiss in annoyance and duck back down, just in time to avoid a bullet puncturing the wall of bottles behind us. More glass and liquid rain down to my left.

"Grifter!"

"I'm fine!" I call back. "Go!"

She doesn't bother to respond. Is it my imagination, or do I hear a siren in the distance?

I grab the nearest screw-top bottle of Everclear from the shelf. I heft it experimentally. Small enough to toss, but large enough to contain a good amount of booze. Highly flammable booze.

"What are you doing?" George wheezes.

"Oh, you know," I say, pulling off my hightop and sock. "Improvising."

I pop up and down again to gauge the distance, like some frenetic whack-a-mole. Bad-cop is too far for a direct hit, but I don't want that anyway. I just want to distract him long enough for us to rush the door.

I open the bottle and stuff my sock all the way in, soaking it in the liquid. Then I pull it out just enough to make a short fuse. I put my shoe back on my sockless foot, so I'm ready to run the second I lob this thing. I light the sock, wait for it to catch enough to reach the lip of the bottle, and then heave myself up and launch the bottle with all my strength.

It crashes to the floor a few feet from Trent. The flames aren't as impressive as if the bottle had been filled with gasoline, but they still make enough of a deterrent that Trent backs further down the aisle. I haul George to his feet and tug him by his uninjured arm. He stumbles after me.

Sadly, Trent isn't as cowed by the flames as I hoped he'd be. He's tracking us down the far aisle on the other side of the rows of shelves. Our only advantage is that the store isn't large. I reach the door handle while Trent is still two rows behind us.

As I push the door wide, I spot Han crouched down behind the row of shelves nearest to the door. Trent will reach her position before he gets to me and George. And she's distracted, reloading her gun.

I can't call out and risk giving away our own position, so I shove George through the open door and whisper-hiss at him to take cover. Then I turn on my heel and make a beeline for Han, barreling into her before she even has a chance to look up.

We hit the floor with a *fwump* just as bad-cop rounds the corner and fires a shot. The bullet misses us but her hand hits the floor with the clatter of her gun skittering off in Trent's direction. A box of wine bottles behind us explodes. Too close. Far too close.

Han rolls out from under me and rushes Trent in a whirlwind of what appear to be knives. Trent drops his gun in the scuffle, and I dive to secure it. He tries to kick it away, but his foot connects with my wrist rather than the gun.

"Ouch! Asshole," I say, as my fingers close around the gun. I automatically flip on the safety, scores of shooting lessons with Dani reeling on a loop in my mind.

Suddenly, Trent turns tail and runs, hopping through a window that had broken in the melee. And, yep, those are definitely sirens now.

"You saved me," Han says, utterly pissed off.

"Yes, how dare I do anything so offensive as keep you alive?" I say, getting to my feet.

"The last thing I want is to owe you anything."

"You don't," I tell her as I grab her wrist and yank her toward the door. "You saved me from the Albanians, remember? We're even."

She twists out of my grip. "I didn't do that for you."

I sigh in aggravation and grab her arm instead, dragging her ungrateful ass to the door. "Go. The cops will be here any minute."

"Don't tell me what to—"

"Leave now. Argue later."

"But—"

"Mike will drive me home."

And mercifully, she finally listens.

THREE HOURS and several rounds of questioning later, Mike and Sam finally arrive at the police station to collect me.

Mike bursts into the mostly concrete and metal room I'm waiting in, the pitiful excuse for coffee they gave me on the small table in front of me. I'm relieved to see him, despite the look of aggravated disappointment he shoots at me.

"Agent Ramirez?" the Internal Affairs officer—something something Delaney—says and gets to his feet.

"They tortured me for hours," I say, indicating the horrible coffee. "Don't worry, I didn't tell them anything."

"Julep," Mike says, his tone the soft and patient one that means he's only barely resisting the urge to strangle me. "I distinctly remember Sam telling you to not do anything dangerous."

"He didn't say that exactly. Where is Sam, anyway?"

"Pacing in the lobby. And if you think *I'm* in a state…"

I wave at him dismissively. "I'm fine. I told you, I had a plan."

"Your plan was to Molotov a liquor store?"

"I never admitted to that," I say, shooting a meaningful glance toward Officer Delaney.

"Agent Ramirez," Delaney says, breaking in. "Julep has given us an account of everything that happened. Enough that I think we can finally close the book on a years-old cold case..."

I straighten in my seat, pleased with the praise.

"...And charge her with reckless public endangerment," Delaney adds acerbically.

I wilt a little at that. I'm pretty sure there's no such thing as a charge of reckless public endangerment, but it wouldn't be the first time a new rule with compensatory punishment was enacted because of something I'd done. St. Agatha's student handbook is full of them.

"But since she saved a life in the process, I think we can let her go with a warning," he finishes, and I sag in relief. He's referring to George, not Han. Han, at least, managed to get away clean. "As long as she leaves Detroit now and doesn't come back."

"Hey," I object. "I didn't shoot up a liquor store."

"Trent Johnson is already in custody and has a lot more coming his way than exile."

"He's the officer who killed Carmen Walker and then covered up the murder?" Mike asks.

"Allegedly," Delaney says, but his eyes confirm it.

"Is she free to go?" Mike moves toward my chair, as if fearful the answer might be no, and he'll have to physically extricate me from the precinct.

"For now," Delaney says. "But we'll likely have follow-up questions."

No doubt they'll have a three-mile list of follow-up questions, once they watch the security footage and see me launching myself at the "unknown gunwoman" trading shots with Trent. But for now, I'm just a bystander.

I get up and trail Mike out to the lobby, where an enraged Sam silently glowers at me. I return his glare with a sheepish smile, but he doesn't relent. Which is hardly fair. It's not like I intended to show up at the same time as bad-cop. It was just good luck.

Once we're belted into Mike's SUV, Mike starts in.

"If I had any hair left, it would all be gray, thanks to you."

"At least, you don't have a heart condition."

"Who says I don't?"

"What were you thinking, Julep?" Sam interrupts from the back. "You should know better than to throw yourself into something like this without backup."

"I had backup!" I protest.

"An enforcer who'd just as soon see you out of the picture than in it does not count as backup!"

He has a point there, but I'm not admitting it. So I segue to revelations to distract him.

"The only explanation that makes any sense with what we now know is that Curran was on the force at the same time as Trent Johnson," I say. "He must have been suspicious of the coroner's ruling Carmen's death an accident."

"With Johnson mucking up Carmen's case from the inside, it would have been hard for Curran to prove. Especially if the bastard had help," Mike adds.

"My theory is that Curran couldn't let it go. He'd become obsessed with solving Carmen's murder. So when the PD closed the case, he kept investigating on his own."

"And it took eight years?" Sam pointed out. "Why escalate it now? How did catfishing as Carmen provoke Johnson to go after Carmen's husband?"

"Curran must have suspected George Walker was involved in his wife's death. That's why he concocted this catfishing plan, to lure out whatever information George might have had."

"That's not a direct line to Johnson," Sam says.

"No, but see, Curran was right about the why—just not the who."

"What do you mean?" Mike interjects.

"Curran suspected that someone from a local syndicate was embedded in the department, and that Carmen found out who it was. He suspected it was someone from George's old crew, that George was involved, and that Carmen found out about it from George."

"But George wasn't involved."

"George told me that Carmen was upset that day by something a student had told her, and that she was going to do something about it that night. She must have been going to report Trent Johnson after his kid ratted him out to Carmen."

"But she never got the chance," Sam says.

"Johnson silenced her and covered it up before she could," Mike concludes.

"Any idea what Johnson was doing?" Sam asks.

"No," I admit. "But I'm sure it's something obvious and cliché—drugs, bribery, extortion, capitalism. Pick your poison. Anyway, that's up to Internal Affairs to suss out. Our job is done. We've caught the catfish."

I experience a sudden pang for George. Poor guy doesn't deserve to have his love ripped away from him twice in one lifetime. I know a little something about how that feels and I don't recommend it.

"What's going to happen to Curran?" Sam asks. "The Detroit PD is not going to love that he was operating so far outside his jurisdiction."

Mike shrugs. "Depends on how much of an in he still has at the PD. His methods were definitely questionable, but he didn't technically break any laws."

"What are you going to tell Anton?" Sam asks me.

I'm already dialing his number when I answer.

"The truth about his mom," I say, wishing that someday, someone would do the same for me.

"WOULD you have scrubbed my file if I'd gone into WITSEC?" I ask Mike later that night as we sit at the kitchen table over a nightcap coffee. We've just confessed the whole messy affair to Angela, who uncharacteristically begged off for bed before we got to the thrilling heroics on my part, claiming a headache.

"If it kept you safe," he answers quietly, "then, yes."

I mull that over. That he'd be willing to do something illegal for me is a heavier responsibility than I was prepared for. The others, sure. But Mike isn't like us. He cares about justice. About the system. About law and righteousness and quantifiable truth. For him to lie for me feels wrong. Dangerous in a way that's different than I'm used to. Like he's risking more than just his job. I find it unsettling.

"I looked into Brillion like you asked," he says, rousing me from my ruminations. "You're not going to like this."

He reaches for his nearby briefcase, opens it, and takes out a file folder. He hesitates, his thinking face warring with his worried face, before he slides it across the table toward me. It's completely flat, which means there's not much information inside.

Heart thudding in my ears, I flip the cover open to see a single sheet of paper. The page is a typed, double-spaced page of text with every word redacted in rigid blocks of black ink. Every word, that is, except one toward the bottom of the first paragraph.

Brillion.

Mike gets to his feet and leans across the table toward me, tapping his finger meaningfully on the header of the heavily redacted page.

"Promise me you won't pursue whatever this is. I mean it, Julep." He straightens to his full height, and he looks as serious as a mountain in a lightning storm. "This is outside *my* sphere, which means it's so far outside *your* sphere as to be in a whole other galaxy. Promise me you'll leave this alone."

I swallow and nod. I've never seen him this worried before, not even when there was a contract on my head. He leaves without so much as a good night, taking the stairs slowly, as if he's suddenly exhausted. As if he knows I've just lied to him. Again.

Once he's out of sight, I look to where his finger left a dent in the paper. A logo in the header is circled in red.

It's the seal of the US Defense Intelligence Agency.

The End

ONE MORE CASE closed for Julep and crew, but the hunt for Dani and the solution to the mystery of the blue-fairy flash drive continue in the next installment *Trust Me, I'm Trying* (geni.us/TrustMeImTrying).

If you enjoyed this story, please leave a review! Reviews help other readers find great stories, which in turn keeps authors in business. The best way to help your favorite authors write their next book is to leave a review of their last one!

To be notified when future Trust Me books are released, sign up for email updates at geni.us/theunder ground.

ABOUT THE AUTHOR

MARY ELIZABETH SUMMER (she/her 🇺🇸) likes to poke at dark places until the light spills out, which is why her characters are constantly glaring at her and applying adhesive bandages. She is currently contributing to the delinquency of minors by writing books about a teen con artist solving mysteries by doing crime. She lives in Portland, Oregon with her daughter and small menagerie of pets. For email updates on new releases, sign up on maryelizabethsummer.com.

amazon.com/author/maryelizabethsummer

instagram.com/mesummerbooks

bsky.app/profile/mesummerbooks.bsky.social

bookbub.com/authors/mary-elizabeth-summer